SECRET SCHOOL INVASION

PAMELA BUTCHART

nosy crow

Look out for:

BABY ALIENS GOT MY TEACHER!

THE SPY WHO LOVED SCHOOL DINNERS

MY HEADTEACHER IS A VAMPIRE RAT!

ATTACK OF THE DEMON DINNER LADIES

TO WEE OR NOT TO WEE!

THERE'S A WEREWOLF IN MY TENT!

THE PHANTOM LOLLIPOP MAN!

THERE'S A YETI IN THE PLAYGROUND!

ICARUS WAS RIDICULOUS

THE BROKEN LEG OF DOOM

A MONSTER ATE MY PACKED LUNCH!

For my friend,
Maya Ingram xxx

First published in the UK in 2022 by Nosy Crow Ltd
The Crow's Nest, 14 Baden Place,
Crosby Row, London, SE1 1YW, UK

Nosy Crow Eireann Ltd
44 Orchard Grove, Kenmare,
Co Kerry, V93 FY22, Ireland

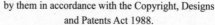

ISBN: 978 1 83994 049 1

A CIP catalogue record for this book will be available from the British Library.

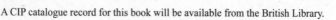

Printed and bound in Great Britain by Clays Ltd, Elcograf S.p.A.

Papers used by Nosy Crow are made from wood grown in sustainable forests.

MIX
Paper from
responsible sources
FSC
www.fsc.org   FSC® C018072

1 2 3 4 5 6 7 8 9 10
www.nosycrow.com

Contents

No One's Shoes Should Ever Be THAT Shiny!

A **LOT** of **WEIRD STUFF** happens at our school. But this was **DIFFERENT**. Because we knew that **THIS** could be the **END OF EVERYTHING**. And it had to do with loads of **NEW PUPILS** and the **FAKEST SMILES EVER** and **EVIL BLAZERS**.

1

But it was when we heard them chanting in a SECRET LANGUAGE that we KNEW things were

NEVER

going to be the same at our school EVER AGAIN.

And we probably should have realised that the SECOND all the new pupils MARCHED into our school because, like my friend Zach says, NO ONE should be able to sing THAT loud.

But it was when one of us went DEEP UNDERCOVER that things got OUT OF CONTROL. Because we didn't KNOW that sometimes when you go undercover you can go TOO DEEP and NEVER come back…

Emergency
Assembly

When we got to school on Monday something

SERIOUSLY WEIRD

was going on. The teachers were NOWHERE

4

to be seen and Gary Petrie was doing highland dancing on top of the old bike shed, shouting, "Come up and join me if you think you're hard enough!" and no one was even trying to stop him.

I was just about to say we should probably go and fetch someone before Gary fell off and broke both his legs when we heard a SCREAM coming from the school office.

We RAN over to see what had happened and that's when we saw that the office ladies were all on the phones SHOUTING about something.

One of them spotted us standing there so

I started to ask what the SCREAM was about but that's when she pulled a little curtain over the glass window really fast, even though I was MID-SENTENCE. (And I never even knew that there WAS a little curtain!)

Then, all of a sudden, loads of teachers came rushing down the corridor towards us and they started knocking on the head teacher's door really hard and they looked

MEGA ANGRY.

We all watched as the door opened just a little bit and then an ARM came out and put a sign on the door. And then the arm disappeared and the door shut really quickly.

I looked at Jodi and Jodi looked at Zach and Zach looked at Maisie but Maisie's eyes had gone all swirly because the sign said:

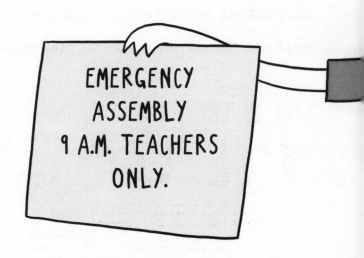

EMERGENCY
ASSEMBLY
9 A.M. TEACHERS
ONLY.

We had

NO IDEA

what was going on because the last time there was a TEACHERS-ONLY emergency assembly was when one of the Year 2s got stuck in the basketball cupboard for half a day because no one could find the key. And we all thought that he was going to have to LIVE IN THERE and drink water and soup through the KEYHOLE with a STRAW for the rest of his life. But a FIRE ENGINE had come and the fire brigade broke down the

door with an AXE and we all got an

EXTRA-LONG

afternoon break.

So I said that we should check to see if someone had got stuck inside the basketball cupboard, but Jodi grabbed my arm and said, "No. This is something else. This is SERIOUS."

And she was RIGHT because the teachers looked MUCH more upset than they had about the Year 2 pupil and Mr Beattie even looked like he was going to cry!

And that's when Jodi's eyes went WIDE and she said, "The Den. Now. RUN!"

So we ran.

We ran along the corridor to The Den (which is our secret place under the stairs that go up to the boys' toilets). But when we got to the end of the corridor there was another SCREAM and the staffroom door FLEW open and MORE teachers came RUSHING out.

Jodi stuck her arms out to the side and PINNED me and Maisie against the wall and yelled, "BREATHE IN!" And we did because we were scared we were going to get TRAMPLED TO DEATH.

I shut my eyes TIGHT as all the teachers

ran past us and I could actually feel **WIND** in my face – that's how fast they were running.

Once the teachers had passed, Jodi said, "**CLEAR**," and dropped her arms, and that's when I let out my breath and when Maisie slid down the wall and on to the floor because she'd fainted.

We got down on our hands and knees and put Maisie in the **RECOVERY POSITION**. We know how to do that because Maisie faints a **LOT** when she gets scared and when she wakes up she always needs a **RIBENA** or a **TWIX** or sometimes **BOTH** if she's had a really big shock.

But then Jodi GASPED and yelled,

"MAN DOWN!
MAN DOWN!"

At first I thought she was talking about Maisie but then I looked and saw that ZACH was curled up in a ball against the wall!

We rushed over and asked if he was OK, and that's when Zach uncurled himself and blinked LOADS and said, "I don't know. I think so. What's HAPPENING?!"

I looked at Jodi and she looked at me and

13

then she said, "Change of plan. There's no time to get to The Den. We need to get to the emergency assembly **NOW**."

So I reminded Jodi that the assembly was for **TEACHERS ONLY**.

And that's when Jodi stood up and put her hands on her hips and said, "The rules no longer apply!"

And I **GASPED** and so did Zach because Jodi only says that in **EXTREMELY SERIOUS** situations, like the time we had to hold Maisie's head up and pretend that she hadn't fainted when she definitely **HAD** because you are not allowed to go on the

Ghost Train if you have fainted, even if you've waited in the queue for over an hour.

So anyway, Zach got up and we all picked Maisie up by the legs and arms and we ran all the way to the assembly hall.

It was  **CHAOS**

when we got to the hall.

The assembly had already started and all the teachers were **SHOUTING OUT** even though we are **NOT ALLOWED** to shout

out in assembly and Mr Graves was telling everyone to

CALM DOWN.

Then one of the dinner ladies actually CLIMBED up on to the stage and GRABBED the microphone out of Mr Graves's hand and yelled, "UNTIL FURTHER NOTICE WE ARE ON STRIKE!"

Then she dropped the microphone on to the floor and LEAPED off the stage and all the dinner ladies cheered and started BANGING their ICE-CREAM SCOOPS on the serving trays.

I looked at Jodi and she said something but I couldn't hear what it was because of all the NOISE.

Mr Graves bent down and picked up the microphone and said, "PLEASE STOP THAT BANGING."

So the dinner ladies stopped. And then they reached up and SLAMMED their metal shutters down.

Zach

and said, "What are we going to eat at lunchtime? I'm STARVING!"

I had

NO IDEA

what we were going to eat for lunch if the dinner ladies were all on STRIKE, but I knew that that was probably the LEAST of our problems because it was only 9 a.m. And also because something BAD was obviously happening but we just didn't know WHAT yet.

Then one of the teachers stood up on a

chair and yelled, "We have to do something! We're all at RISK!"

And then loads of the other teachers started shouting out at the same time and Mr Graves looked like he was going to be sick.

Jodi grabbed my arm and SQUEEZED and I knew that she did it because Miss Ross had just said that we were all AT RISK.

And that's when Mr Graves said,

"EVERYONE, PLEASE!
CALM DOWN.
THE CHILDREN WILL HEAR!"

And then one of the other teachers said, "They deserve to know! This affects them too!"

And that's when Jodi gasped and said, "THIS IS NOT A DRILL!"

And I felt a bit dizzy but I just took a deep breath and nodded.

Because that is our CODE for when something is SERIOUSLY WRONG.

999!

The next day Mr Graves called us all to an assembly and told us that ANOTHER school was going to be joining OUR school and that we were going to be

ONE BIG HAPPY SCHOOL.

We were all in SHOCK when he said that and we just sat with our mouths WIDE OPEN because none of us knew what to say because it didn't make any sense!

Then Mr Graves took a deep breath and asked us if we had any questions and ALL the teachers put their hands up and Mr Graves closed his eyes and took a deep breath and said, "Questions from the PUPILS."

But Mr Killington kept his hand up in the air and his face looked a bit like it was going to

if Mr Graves didn't pick him!

That's when one of the Year 6s put up their hand and asked which school was going to be joining us, and Mr Graves took another deep breath and said, "St Balthazar's Primary School."

And as SOON as he said that we all

GASPED.

I looked at Jodi and she looked at me but neither of us said anything because we were in

SHOCK.

And we were in

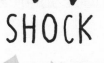
SHOCK

because St Balthazar's and our school are

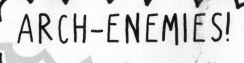
ARCH-ENEMIES!

Zach grabbed my arm and said, "This can't

happen. We can't let this happen. They're

EVIL!"

And I nodded loads.

All the teachers had started whispering to each other and Miss Jones even looked a bit scared!

Then another Year 6 asked how many pupils would be coming to our school and everyone went SILENT and Mr Graves looked nervous.

We all watched as Mr Graves took a bit of paper out of his folder and said, "Um. Well, I just got the information this morning and I've not had a chance to share it with the staff or your parents yet. And at the moment the numbers are changing daily... But ... um ... the number today is one hundred and two."

And that's when the teachers went

MAD

and started YELLING at Mr Graves about
CLASSROOM SIZES and RESOURCES
and CHAIRS and Mr Killington actually got
up and shouted, "I'm going home!" And
then he WALKED OUT.

Everyone GASPED, especially the Year 6s,
because Mr Killington is THEIR teacher so
that meant that they had NO TEACHER.

Loads of the Year 6s got up and ran over to the window and yelled, "He's really leaving! He's getting in his car!"

Then some of the Year 6 girls started crying and hugging each other and the teachers kept shouting and Mr Graves kept trying to calm everyone down. And it was

CHAOS.

But then suddenly everyone went quiet because we could all hear something.

And it sounded a bit like MARCHING.

Mr Graves gasped and whispered, "They're

here. Save us all."

And I knew that we weren't supposed to hear him say that and that he'd forgotten he was standing in front of a microphone!

I looked at Jodi and she had Zach's phone in her hand and I could see that she'd already dialled

and that she had her finger hovering over the CALL BUTTON.

I could feel myself starting to

PANIC

as the marching got LOUDER and LOUDER because I just KNEW that it was THEM.

Mr Graves tried to say something into the microphone but his voice came out all high and weird. So he cleared his throat and then he said, "Children. Would you please welcome the St Balthazar's School Choir. They're going to do a performance for us to mark the wonderful occasion of two schools coming together!"

And then he RAN off the stage.

We all sat STUNNED in TOTAL SILENCE as rows and rows of pupils with BLAZERS and SUPER-SHINY SHOES marched into the hall and up the little steps on to the stage.

Then they stopped suddenly and turned to us and smiled

HUGE CREEPY SMILES

at EXACTLY the same time and everyone

GASPED, even the teachers, and Maisie gripped my hand so tight I almost screamed!

Then, all of a sudden, they BURST out singing REALLY LOUD and everyone GASPED because it sounded

SUPER CREEPY

and Maisie's head fell into my lap because she'd fainted INSTANTLY and Jodi pressed "CALL" on Zach's phone and held it up in the air so the POLICE could hear.

DOPPELGANGERS

Once the police had left and Maisie had gone off with the school nurse, Mr Graves gave me and Jodi and Zach a TALK about how we should NEVER call the police unless it was an ACTUAL EMERGENCY.

So that's when Jodi explained that it WAS

AN ACTUAL EMERGENCY

and that the singing had been so TERRIFYING that two of the Year 1s had been physically SICK.

That's when Mr Graves sighed and rubbed his face for ages and said, "Just go back to class. We'll talk about this later."

So we ran out because we HATE being sent to the head teacher's office. My dad says that if we hate it so much then we should try NOT doing the things that get us sent there. But that doesn't really

make much sense because we're only ever trying to SAVE our school. And I think that in the future when we're all old (like about thirty or something) we are actually going to star in a film or a DOCUMENTARY about how AMAZINGLY USEFUL we were.

So anyway, we ran to see the nurse before we went to class to see if Maisie had woken up yet and if she was OK and if we could take her back to class. But the nurse said that Maisie needed to stay and rest.

We asked if we could see her but the nurse said no.

So I shouted,

"WE'RE HERE, MAISIE!
WE LOVE YOU!
WE'LL BE BACK AT BREAK
WITH YOUR TWIX!
DO YOU NEED ANYTHING ELSE?"

But then the nurse shut the door so we didn't get to hear Maisie's reply.

When we got to the classroom we BURST through the door. And then we FROZE. And Zach GASPED. Because there were FOUR

37

NEW PUPILS sitting at our table. And they were sitting in OUR seats!

We had

NO IDEA

what to do so we just stood there STARING at them and they STARED back at us and it was OBVIOUS that they didn't even CARE that they'd stolen our seats! Then Miss Jones came over and told us to sit on the floor and not make a "FUSS" about it. Which I thought was a bit unfair because we hadn't even said ONE WORD, so it was like we were getting told off for something we hadn't even DONE yet!

Then Miss Jones said, "Everyone, I know this isn't ideal."

And then she laughed a bit to herself (which was weird because it wasn't funny and also because her laugh didn't sound **ANYTHING** like her normal laugh).

I looked at Jodi and Jodi looked at me because it was obvious Miss Jones was

FREAKING OUT.

Then Miss Jones cleared her throat and stopped laughing and said, "There obviously isn't enough space for everyone at the moment. But as soon as we open up the Old Wing, we'll have plenty of room."

That's when we all looked at each other and Gary Petrie shouted, "**WHAT?**"

And Miss Jones told him off for shouting out.

So Gary Petrie put his hand up and said,

And Miss Jones closed her eyes for a second and then she opened them and said, "I said, we're opening up the Old Wing, Gary."

And Gary Petrie said, "That old bit next to the boys' toilets? But it's all boarded up!"

I turned to Jodi and whispered, "That's where The Den is!"

And Jodi nodded loads.

That's when Miss Jones explained that there were actually FOUR EXTRA CLASSROOMS in the Old Wing and that it had been closed off for years to save money on electricity and carpets because we didn't need the space.

And then she said, "But now that we're

we can put those classrooms to good use."

Everyone was

SHOCKED

and LOADS of people kept putting their hands up and asking questions about the

"SECRET SCHOOL"

in the Old Wing and if the classrooms were better than ours and how LONG it had been shut for and if there were was anything ELSE in there.

But Miss Jones said that she didn't know

and that it had been CLOSED OFF since before she was a teacher.

That's when one of the new pupils sitting at our old table put his hand up and Miss Jones said, "Yes. Zavier, isn't it? Am I pronouncing that correctly?"

We all turned around and looked at Zavier.

Zavier smiled and said, "Yes, Miss. We can't wait for the new wing to open. And for our old teachers to get here. We're all going to be one big happy family!"

And then he gave Miss Jones a

HUGE CREEPY SMILE.

But Miss Jones didn't smile back. Well, she did a bit but it wasn't like her normal smile and she looked like she had a pain somewhere.

I looked at Jodi and her eyes were WIDE and I knew that it was because the NEW PUPILS already KNEW about the

SECRET SCHOOL.

Miss Jones started the lesson but I couldn't concentrate because Zach kept turning around and looking over at our old table and he had a REALLY WEIRD look on his face.

Then he leaned over to me and whispered, "Do you notice anything about the new pupils at our table?"

So I turned round and looked. I couldn't see it at first but then, JUST as I was about to turn back, I realised something that made me

GASP.

One of the new girls sitting at our table looked like Jodi! She even had the same HAIR BOBBLE in her hair!

I looked at Zach and whispered, "She looks like Jodi!"

Zach nodded loads and then he said, "Did you notice anything else?"

So I turned round and looked again and that's when I noticed that Zavier looked a bit like Zach but with shorter hair.

I looked at Zach and said, "This is weird."

And that's when Zach nodded and said, "It's about to get even WEIRDER... Look at the girl sitting in YOUR seat!"

So I turned round again but I couldn't see
her properly because she had her back to
us. But then she moved.

And I actually GASPED.

And Zach did a GULP.

She was staring RIGHT AT US.

And she looked EXACTLY LIKE ME!

I turned my head away REALLY FAST
and I actually covered my eyes with my

HANDS because I was

FREAKING OUT.

That's when Jodi moved closer and asked us what was going on and Zach explained and Jodi looked over at the new pupils and back at us, shocked.

Then before we could say anything to

each other the classroom door opened and Maisie walked in.

But then I GASPED.

And Zach GASPED.

Because it WASN'T Maisie.

We all STARED as a small girl with pigtails walked past us and sat down at our old table.

And then Miss Jones said, "Hello. You must be Daisy, yes?"

And I couldn't BELIEVE that she was called Daisy!

But Daisy didn't say anything.

Then the girl who looked EXACTLY like me said, "Yes, Miss. This is Daisy."

Miss Jones asked Daisy if she was OK, but Daisy didn't say anything.

And then the Me Girl said, "Sorry, Miss. Daisy's just a bit shy. She gets scared of new people and new places."

I looked at Jodi and her mouth was actually hanging WIDE OPEN.

Because this was unbelievable.

THEY WERE US!

Victorian Ghosts?

As soon as the bell went, me and Jodi and Zach raced down the stairs and along the corridor to get Maisie because we needed to have an

OFFICIAL MEETING

and we needed to have it

When we got there Maisie was waiting on a little seat outside the nurse's room and she looked really PALE.

So I gave her a carton of Ribena and a Twix because she'd obviously had a horrible shock. Maisie took a drink of juice and a bite of the Twix and then she looked up at us and said, "Have they gone yet?"

And we all knew that she meant the NEW PUPILS.

So that's when I said that they were still here but that they'd stopped singing so that was better and Maisie did a little nod and a bit of a whimper.

Then Jodi said, "It's time. Let's go."

So we all **RAN** along the corridor to The Den because we knew we needed to have a

SECRET MEETING ASAP.

But on the way we heard **SHOUTING** coming from the playground so we rushed

out to see what was going on and **THAT'S** when we saw that the new pupils had completely **TAKEN OVER** the playground!

Gary Petrie was going **MENTAL** because he wanted to play football like he **ALWAYS** does at break but there wasn't any space because the new pupils were playing some sort of handball game.

That's when Jodi said, "Look at how many of them there are! More must have arrived!"

And then Zach said, "Look at how good they are at throwing that ball. It's going for miles!"

That's when Zach **GASPED**.

And Jodi said, "What?"

But Zach said, "Not here. It's not SECURE. Let's get to The Den."

So we all ran along to The Den and when we got there Jodi made sure we hadn't been followed and then she shut the door and got the whiteboard and the pen out and Zach poured us all a cup of cold tea while we told Maisie about the other pupils looking like us.

Zach always makes the tea because there's a sink and an old kettle and some leftover teabags in The Den from when it used to be the old janitor's hiding place. But we just have our tea cold because the kettle doesn't work and we don't have any milk and we usually just hold our tea and don't drink it because none of us really likes tea anyway.

But this time, Zach actually started **DRINKING** his and he said that it was because he needed to **CALM DOWN** and that his mum always had a cup of tea when she needed to calm down.

Then Jodi said that the meeting had

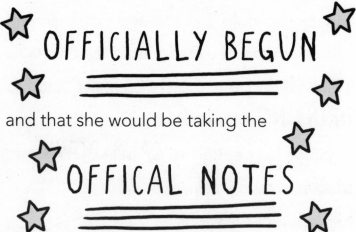

OFFICIALLY BEGUN

and that she would be taking the

OFFICAL NOTES

and that we would all get a copy the next day once she'd had a chance to write out three copies at home. And that once we had read them we had to DESTROY them and that she would keep ONE COPY ONLY in the metal pencil case that we kept under the loose floorboard in The Den. And we all nodded.

Then she looked at Zach and said, "Go."

And we all knew that Jodi wanted Zach to tell us why he had

when we were watching the NEW PUPILS in the playground and that she wanted him to tell us QUICKLY (because Jodi doesn't like not knowing things and she definitely doesn't like waiting).

Zach took a deep breath but then Maisie

yelled, "VICTORIAN GHOSTS!"

Then Maisie started SHAKING and saying loads of stuff about how the new pupils looked TOO CREEPY and that their BLAZERS made them look like they were from OLDEN TIMES and that the choir had sounded

TOO GHOSTLY.

I looked at Jodi and she could tell that I was starting to

PANIC

because ghosts are my WORST THING and when we had to deal with a PHANTOM LOLLIPOP MAN at our school I didn't think that I would COPE.

That's when Jodi said that she didn't think they WERE ghosts, even though the singing had been totally creepy and that she thought they were definitely ALIVE.

But she wrote VICTORIAN GHOSTS down on the whiteboard anyway because we couldn't rule ANYTHING out until we'd done a

THOROUGH INVESTIGATION.

Then we all looked at Zach and Zach took a deep breath and Maisie SQUEEZED my hand really tightly.

And that's when Zach said, "I don't think they're ghosts. But I don't think they're

humans either."

THE INCIDENT

We all sat there **STARING** at Zach because
we couldn't **BELIEVE** what he'd just said!
And then Jodi said, "**MORE**," and Zach's eyes
went **WIDE** and he said, "It's **TOO WEIRD**
that they look so much like us. Especially the
one who looks like Izzy!"

And I nodded loads because it was

REALLY FREAKING
ME OUT!

Then Zach said, "And we all saw how far they can throw a ball. I mean, that's not normal, is it? They're **TOO STRONG**."

I had

NO IDEA

what Zach was trying to tell us and I could see that Jodi was starting to get a bit

ANNOYED at how long it was taking Zach to explain because one of her **EYES** had started to **TWITCH**.

But then Zach said, "I think the new pupils might be **CLONES**."

I looked at Jodi and she'd stopped twitching and her eyes were **WIDE**.

That's when Zach stood up and started walking around and waving his arms about and saying, "It all makes sense! St Balthazar's

must have been some sort of

WEIRD SCIENCE EXPERIMENT."

Zach was speaking REALLY FAST and saying loads of stuff like "EXACT COPIES OF US" and "ARMY OF CLONES" and "SUPER-STRENGTH".

Then he said, "It explains the MARCHING and the SHINY SHOES. They're an army of

SUPER PUPILS

and they've come to REPLACE US!"

So Jodi wrote

> ## "ARMY OF CLONES COME TO REPLACE US"

on the whiteboard and held it up for us to

see but that made Maisie SCREAM

so I had to cover her mouth

until she stopped

because no one is

supposed to

know about

The Den.

Then Jodi said that she wasn't sure about the CLONE THING and then she wrote down something ELSE on the whiteboard and held it up for us to see and it said:

"SOMETHING TO DO WITH THE INCIDENT"

That's when Maisie started SHAKING and she said, "What is THE INCIDENT?!"

And I remembered that Maisie didn't KNOW about

because she wasn't there when it happened.

I always forget that she didn't join our school until halfway through Year 2!

Maisie stared up at me with HUGE EYES and said,

"WAIT! IS IT SCARY?!
DON'T TELL ME IF IT'S SCARY!"

So I took Maisie's hand and patted it and told her not to worry and that it wasn't scary. And then we all told Maisie about

THE INCIDENT

and how our school had entered the same SINGING COMPETITION as St Balthazar's and that BOTH school choirs had been on the LOCAL RADIO and how WE had won and got a BIG TROPHY and were on the TV and everything! And how St Balthazar's had said THEY should have won and that THEY were much better singers. And then how the trophy had

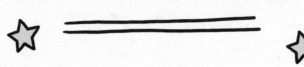

MYSTERIOUSLY DISAPPEARED

and that everyone KNEW St Balthazar's had snuck into our school and STOLEN IT.

And then Jodi said, "And that's why we're enemies. And now they're here. With their CHOIR. They're EVIL and I don't trust them and it's up to US to find out what they're up to!"

Shepherd's Pie Lie

As soon as we got to the dining hall, things got

It was shepherd's pie day so we'd brought

packed lunches but they got taken off us at the dining-hall door just like they ALWAYS do because we are not allowed to bring a packed lunch just because we don't like the shepherd's pie.

And even though we have done

LOADS

of stuff, like write a letter to the COUNCIL and the PARENTS AND CARERS ASSOCIATION and even the POLICE, the dinner ladies just keep serving it.

So anyway, we all went up and got our

shepherd's pie and sat down at our tables and ate it really fast while holding our noses and drinking loads of water like we always do so we don't have to taste it as much.

Then when we finished Jodi had ACTUAL TEARS in her eyes. That's how bad it had been!

And that's when our WHOLE TABLE started to SHAKE. And it was shaking because Maisie's WHOLE BODY was shaking!

Then Maisie said, "Look!"

So we looked where she was looking and that's when we saw it.

ALL the new pupils were eating the shepherd's pie and they were LICKING THEIR LIPS and saying, "OH YUM!"

We all GASPED and Jodi said, "That is NOT OK."

And I shook my head LOADS because it DEFINITELY WASN'T because the shepherd's pie at our school tastes like

SOAPY FEET

and it's all watery and BUMPY and the dinner ladies serve it with an ICE-CREAM SCOOP that they never wash.

Then, all of a sudden, EVERY SINGLE new pupil got to their feet and went up for SECONDS.

That's when Jodi got a really weird look on her face.

Once we got back to class Jodi looked at Zach and said, "I still think you're wrong about the clone thing. I mean, they DO look like us, but they don't look EXACTLY like us."

And that's when Maisie squealed, "Victorian ghosts!"

Jodi shook her head and leaned in close and whispered, "No. I don't think they're clones or ghosts or anything like that. But I do think they're

FAKERS."

And then she said, "We need to talk about

THE SHEPHERD'S PIE."

And Maisie started shaking her head LOADS and she pulled her knees up to her chest and shaking rocking backwards and forwards and whimpering a bit because Maisie HATES it when we even TALK about the shepherd's pie, that's how

DISGUSTING it is.

But Jodi said that she thought they were obviously

FAKERS

because the shepherd's pie is disgusting and also because it sounded really WEIRD the way they kept shouting

and how they all went up for seconds at the same time.

And then she said, "It was like they'd

PLANNED it. Like a scene from a film or something. I don't think they loved it, I think they just wanted the dinner ladies to THINK they loved it."

Then, JUST as Jodi said that, the girl who looked a lot like Jodi got up and walked RIGHT over to us and said, "Are you talking about us?"

Jodi looked completely shocked and then she said, "Um … no."

The girl put her hands on her hips like Jodi always does and then she looked at us all

ONE BY ONE

and said, "What were you talking about then?"

I STARED at Jodi because she is really good at coming up with things on the spot (like the time we got caught trying to free the Year 1 hamster) but Jodi wasn't saying anything! She was just sitting there with a really weird look on her face.

So I knew that I had to say something so that's when I blurted out, "Shepherd's pie!"

The girl STARED at me but she didn't say anything. I could just TELL that she was trying to figure out if I was telling the truth or not.

Then Jodi's face started working again and she said, "Did you all like the shepherd's pie?"

And that's when the girl's face completely changed and she looked at Jodi and did a great big

and said, "Yeah! It was great! You're all soooooooooo lucky to have such great shepherd's pie here. And the dinner ladies are lovely!"

I looked at Zach and Zach looked at me

because the shepherd's pie is **NOT** great and we'd

never heard anyone call the dinner ladies **LOVELY** before!

Jodi's eyes went **WIDE**.

And then she smiled and said, "Yes, they are lovely. And we are lucky, thank you."

Then the girl said, "I'm Jessi, by the way. And that's Zavier, Daisy and Mika. And you're Jodi, Zach, Maisie and Izzy, aren't you?"

And then before we could even answer she

smiled a FAKE SMILE and walked away.

I STARED at Jodi because I couldn't believe that she knew all our names already! It was so weird!

But Jodi wasn't staring back. She just opened her book and got on with her work. Then, after a minute, Jodi pushed her book towards me and then she put her hand up and asked to go to the toilet. And that's when I looked and saw that she HADN'T been doing her work and that she had been writing a NOTE to us instead!

And it said:

THEY'RE ACTING.
THEY'RE PRETENDING
THEY LIKE THE
SHEPHERD'S PIE.
THEY FOUND OUT OUR
NAMES WITHOUT US
TELLING THEM.
THEY ARE DEFINITELY UP
TO SOMETHING.
WE NEED TO FIND OUT
WHAT IT IS.
MEET ME IN THE TOILET
DESTROY THIS PAGE!

Who Flushed the Toilet?!

When I got to the toilets they were empty and I started to get a bit freaked out because everyone knows that the girls' toilets at our school are

HAUNTED.

I was just about to leave when Jodi hissed, "Izzy! Over here!"

And I saw that Jodi's head was peeking over the top of one of the cubicles.

I rushed over and Jodi jumped down and unlocked the door and let me in.

Then she said, "Sit down. We need to talk about

THE INCIDENT."

So I put the toilet lid down and then I laid loads of toilet roll across the seat before I sat down because it looked all dusty and horrible.

And that's when Jodi said, "What do you remember about it?"

So then I told her that I remembered

because it's not every day another school breaks into your SCHOOL and steals your TROPHY!

Jodi bent down and looked me RIGHT in the eyes and said, "Do you remember the NOTE?"

And I shook my head because I wasn't sure what Jodi meant. Then, all of a sudden, a MEMORY flashed into my

and I jumped up off the toilet seat and yelled, "I remember! I REMEMBER! They stuck a note to the front of our school bus! On the window!"

And Jodi's eyes went WIDE and she pushed her face close to mine and said, "And do you remember what the note said?"

And then I GASPED because I DID remember.

And Jodi nodded and said, "That's right. It said,

'THIS ISN'T OVER!'"

And we both looked at each other with our eyes WIDE.

But then, all of a sudden, we heard a toilet FLUSH and I GASPED and Jodi put her hand over my mouth and put a finger up to her lips to tell me to stay quiet.

We listened in silence for a minute but I couldn't hear anything except for the sound of my own heart beating really fast in my chest.

Then Jodi quietly climbed up on to the toilet seat and peeked out over the top of the cubicle.

And then she looked down at me and shook her head and whispered, "There's no one here."

And that's when I started to

PANIC

because if no one was there, then that meant that the

TOILET GHOST

must have flushed the toilet!

So before Jodi could stop me I unlocked the door and

RAN.

Miss Veil

The next day, LOADS of NEW TEACHERS arrived. And they ALL looked a bit scary. We were almost late to class because Maisie was so scared that she locked herself in the toilet and Jodi had to climb over the cubicle wall and unlock the door from the inside.

Then when we got to class, we saw that one of them was in OUR classroom and that she was sitting at Miss Jones's desk!

I was panicking a bit and I was just about to ask where Miss Jones was when I looked and saw that Miss Jones was sitting at a NEW DESK at the BACK of the classroom. EVERYONE was

FREAKING OUT

because it was WEIRD having TWO teachers and TWO teachers' desks in ONE classroom!

That's when **BOTH** teachers stood up and said, "Take your seats, please" at **EXACTLY** the same time and we all looked around but no one moved and Miss Jones and the new teacher **STARED** at each other in the **EYES** for **AGES** and they both stayed standing up until eventually the new teacher coughed and sat down and then Miss Jones said, "Please sit, everyone," and everyone sat down in silence.

None of us knew **WHERE** to look because we didn't know who was in **CHARGE** and if we were supposed to be looking at **MISS JONES** at the **BACK** of the classroom or the NEW TEACHER at the FRONT of the classroom.

And that's when Jodi stood up and turned her chair round to face Miss Jones and someone GASPED. But then LOADS of people started doing the same!

Miss Jones started writing something on the little board at the back of the room and asking us to copy it in our notebooks, so we did.

But that's when I noticed that the new pupils weren't even LOOKING and they DEFINITELY weren't writing anything down!

Then the new teacher said, "If you could all look **THIS** way, please, I've written my name on the board for you to copy down at the front of your notebooks."

I looked at Jodi and **GULPED** because I wasn't sure **WHAT** to do because we already had **MISS JONES'S NAME** written at the front of our notebooks! Then Miss Jones said,

"There's no need for that just yet, Miss Veil."

And as SOON as Miss Jones said that, Miss Veil's face went a bit RED and she SLAMMED her pen down on the desk and said, "WELL."

And then she STARED at Miss Jones.

And Miss Jones scowled and STARED BACK.

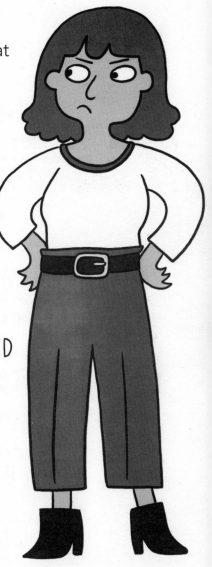

I looked at Jodi and she had her mouth

 WIDE OPEN.

And Zach whispered, "This is WAR."

At break, we heard SHOUTING coming from the STAFFROOM so we sneaked over and listened at the door and that's when we heard Mrs Leppard shouting about how her MUG had been STOLEN.

Then someone else started shouting about a SANDWICH and how it had been MOVED and that their MILK was MISSING.

Then someone said that their

FAVOURITE CHAIR

had GONE.

And that's when we heard Mr Killington

say,

"WE ARE NOT SAFE
IN THIS PLACE ANY MORE."

A Snake Wrapped Round a Donut

That afternoon Jodi said that we needed to watch the new pupils AND their teachers CLOSELY to find out what they were up to.

Jodi said that she thought that if St Balthazar's could steal a TROPHY, they could definitely steal some MILK and a

CHAIR and move a SANDWICH.

So Zach said that we should watch them in SHIFTS so that we could still get our work done because we had TWO teachers now and he didn't want to get into trouble TWICE and that he would take the first shift.

But then, when he had only been doing his shift for five minutes, he said, "I think something's going on!"

That's when Zach told us to look but not look, which is when you DO look at something but you pretend that you're NOT looking so that the person or people you're looking at don't notice that you're looking at them.

So we all looked but didn't look at the new pupils as they walked in and out from being at the library and Zach said, "Do you see it?"

At first I didn't know what he meant but then I noticed that every time they passed each other they touched the BADGE on their BLAZERS.

Zach whispered, "Keep watching. I think they're ALL going to do it!"

So we kept watching until every single new pupil had gone to the library and come back and he was

 RIGHT.

Zach said that he thought it was a

SECRET SIGNAL

and that they were TALKING to each other without ACTUALLY TALKING. And that touching their blazer badge when they passed each other MEANT SOMETHING.

That's when Jodi

GASPED

and put both hands up to her mouth.

And Miss Jones said, "Jodi."

We all thought that Jodi was about to get told off for not doing her work and for **GASPING** really **LOUD** because we often get told off for

TALKING and GASPING

and one time for **SCREAMING**.

But then Miss Jones said, "Would you collect the notebooks please?"

And then Miss Veil said, "Yes, Jodi. I was just about to ask you the same thing."

And Miss Jones gave Miss Veil a **LOOK**.

So Jodi nodded and got up and started collecting everyone's notebooks. But the way she was doing it was WEIRD and we could just TELL that she was in SHOCK because her eyes were HUGE and her mouth was actually hanging open a bit.

I thought I was going to EXPLODE waiting for Jodi to collect all the notebooks and sit back down and tell us what had made her gasp so loud because whatever it was it was obviously

BIG.

But as SOON as the bell went, Jodi just LEFT.

I looked at Zach and Maisie and they were both just as surprised as I was because we had

NO IDEA

why she would just LEAVE WITHOUT US because we ALWAYS leave together at the end of the day.

So we grabbed our coats and ran out after her and that's when we saw that she wasn't even waiting for us in the corridor and that she was GONE!

Then Zach said, "The Den!"

So we all RAN to The Den and when we got there Jodi was waiting for us and she said, "We've got a SERIOUS problem."

We all nodded LOADS and sat down and Jodi said, "Zach was RIGHT. They ARE doing SECRET SIGNALS. I think they've

formed a SECRET SOCIETY."

And we all GASPED.

But then Zach said that secret societies have MORE than just

SECRET SIGNALS

and that they have

SECRET HANDSHAKES

and SECRET SYMBOLS too.

And THAT'S when Jodi's eyes went

wide and she stood up and picked up her backpack and for a second I thought she was about to **LEAVE** because she didn't like what Zach had said.

But then she stepped forward into the middle of our little circle.

And then she turned her backpack upside down and shook it and **LOADS** of notebooks fell on to the floor!

We all gasped but we had

why Jodi had **STOLEN** our class's

NOTEBOOKS.

Then Jodi said, "Pick one, any one!"

So Zach reached forward and picked one up.

And Jodi said, "Look at the bottom left-hand corner."

And Zach looked and said, "What? This?"

And Jodi nodded, so we looked and saw that it was a tiny doodle that looked a bit like a snake wrapped round a donut.

Then Jodi said, "It's a SECRET SYMBOL."

That's when I said that it was definitely WEIRD but that we couldn't tell for sure that it was a SECRET-SOCIETY SYMBOL.

And then Jodi's eyes went even WIDER than they'd been before, which I didn't think was possible!

And she kept looking at me but said, "Zach, why don't you choose another one?"

So Zach leaned forward and picked up another notebook and opened it and I heard him GULP.

And I looked and saw that the notebook had the EXACT same doodle in the EXACT same place.

And then Jodi said, "And before you ask … yes, they're all like that.

"EVERY. SINGLE. LAST. ONE."

Intruder in The Den

The next day, things got even

STRANGER.

Miss Jones looked EXHAUSTED and
then we overheard her tell Mrs Leppard that

she'd got to work at 6am!

We had

NO IDEA

why Miss Jones would come to school when it was still DARK but it obviously had something to do with her car because she kept saying something about "SECURING HER PARKING SPACE" over and over.

Then we overheard Mr Beattie say that he hadn't slept much because he'd been

TRAINING until 2am!

We had

what was going on or what Mr Beattie was TRAINING for. All we knew was that the teachers were acting REALLY WEIRD and Mr Beattie was wearing a TIE and he'd tucked his shirt in properly and EVERYTHING.

At break Jodi said that we needed to have an

URGENT SECRET MEETING

in The Den about what the SECRET SOCIETY were up to and why the teachers were acting so weird.

But as SOON as we walked inside The Den, Jodi FROZE.

Then she said, "Something isn't right."

I looked around to see what was wrong but I couldn't see anything. Everything looked normal.

That's when Jodi said that everything might LOOK normal but that it didn't FEEL normal. At first I thought that Jodi maybe meant that it felt a bit COLDER than it usually did. But then Jodi looked RIGHT at me and said, "Someone was here. I can FEEL IT."

That's when Maisie started shaking VIOLENTLY and screaming,

"GET THEM OUT!
GET THEM OUT!"

We tried to calm her down and I kept telling her over and over that there wasn't anyone in The Den except for us. But Maisie wouldn't open her eyes and she was shaking her head SO FAST that her pigtails were hitting me in the face! Then, all of a sudden, her pigtails stopped swinging and she fainted.

So we put Maisie in the recovery position and covered her with our jackets to keep her warm.

Then Jodi looked at me and Zach with a SERIOUS look on her face and said, "We need to turn this place upside down. NOW."

That's when Jodi explained that she was worried the new pupils had put a

BUGGING DEVICE

in The Den and that she'd seen it on the TRUE CRIME programme she watches with her mum.

So we checked under all the upturned buckets we use as chairs and the sink area, and Jodi even made us open every single book on the bookcase and flick through all the pages TWICE. Then, when she was sure there wasn't a BUGGING DEVICE in

The Den she said, "CLEAR," and we all sat down and I held a Twix under Maisie's nose because sometimes she wakes up when she smells the chocolate.

Jodi said that the meeting had

OFFICIALLY STARTED

and then she pulled up the loose floorboard and took out the pad and pen and started writing something down REALLY FAST.

And when she held it up for us to see, it said:

WHAT WE KNOW ABOUT
THE NEW PUPILS:
THEY ARE FAKING LIKING
THE SHEPHERD'S PIE AND
THE DINNER LADIES
THEY HAVE FORMED A
SECRET SOCIETY
THEY WERE IN THE DEN
THEY'RE SPYING ON US

So that's when I said that we didn't know for SURE they were spying on us.

And Jodi said that we DID.

And I said that we DIDN'T because we didn't have any

EVIDENCE

yet and that we hadn't found any SPY EQUIPMENT.

And then Zach said, "We don't even know for sure that someone WAS in The Den."

And that's when Jodi got REALLY ANNOYED because she doesn't like it when

people don't believe her about stuff.

Then she looked at us and said, **"FINE!"**

And she got down on her hands and knees and started staring at the ground.

Me and Zach looked at each other because we had

what Jodi was doing!

So I got down on my hands and knees too and asked Jodi if she was **OK** and if she was upset at us, and that's when Jodi said that she was looking for **EVIDENCE** that an

INTRUDER might have left behind, like FOOTPRINTS or HAIR.

Zach said, "YUCK. Why would they leave their HAIR?!"

And Jodi said that they wouldn't have left it on PURPOSE and that the average human has about 100,000 hairs on their head and that they lose about 100 a day and that loads of those are lost when you're just walking about.

Then, all of a sudden, Jodi said, "AHA! FOUND SOMETHING!"

And then she held up a **LONG BLACK HAIR** and Zach said, "**YUCK!** Get it away from me!"

Jodi grabbed the torch we keep in The Den in case someone accidentally switches the light out (because the light switch is on the **OUTSIDE** of the door). And then she

127

held up the hair and said that she needed to EXAMINE it CLOSELY for at least three minutes.

I was SURE that it was one of JODI'S hairs because SHE has long black hair. But I didn't say anything because Jodi was already annoyed at us for saying that we didn't believe her.

Then she got a RULER out of her bag and started MEASURING the hair and then she looked at us and said, "I'm 99.9 per cent sure this isn't my hair. It's too long. But we need to cross-check."

And that's when she said that I had to

PULL OUT one of her HAIRS and that I had to make sure I pulled it out at the ROOT so we got the TRUE LENGTH.

And then she took her ponytail down and we all

GASPED

because Jodi NEVER takes her hair down and it made her look like a COMPLETELY DIFFERENT PERSON.

I really didn't want to be the one to pull out one of Jodi's hairs because I didn't want her to be ANGRY at me if it HURT, so I made

Jodi PROMISE that she wouldn't blame me or shout at me if it hurt and she promised that she wouldn't.

So I started looking at the ENDS of Jodi's hair and Jodi started moaning and saying that I was "DOING IT WRONG".

So that's when I said that I WASN'T doing it wrong, actually, and that I was trying to find the LONGEST HAIR she had and then I would follow it all the way up to her head and pull it out at the root like she'd said.

And Jodi didn't say anything because she knew I was right and she's not very good at saying sorry.

When I found the longest hair, I pulled it out as GENTLY as I could.

But Jodi GASPED and then she SCREAMED so loud that Maisie JUMPED under all our jackets and Zach hissed, "Shhhhh! Someone will hear!"

Jodi GRABBED the hair out of my hand and gave me a LOOK (which I didn't think was very fair at all!). But as soon as she held the hair up against the hair she'd found on the ground I could tell that she wasn't annoyed at me any more.

Because the GROUND HAIR was MUCH longer that Jodi's longest hair.

That's when Jodi smiled.

And Zach gasped and said, "Someone WAS in here!"

And Jodi nodded. And then she said, "And now we've got EVIDENCE to prove it!"

The Secret Key!

We were all in SHOCK that someone had been inside The Den!

That's when Zach said, "But how did they get in here?! We're the only ones with a key!"

And he was RIGHT because we thought

we'd lost the key ages ago so we never used to be able to lock The Den door but then Jodi FOUND IT in the bottom of her old school bag and we've been locking the door ever since.

And that's when a little voice said, "There might be another key."

We all looked down and saw that Maisie was still lying on the floor but that she was awake now and had almost finished her Twix.

Maisie looked up at us with her HUGE EYES and she looked a bit like she was going to cry.

And then she said, "I got a copy made."

And we all

because we couldn't believe it!

And then Maisie said, "I was scared that we'd lose it again and wouldn't be able to get inside if it was an emergency and we needed somewhere hide! So I took it out of Jodi's bag when she wasn't looking."

That's when Maisie told us that she'd taken the key to TESCO when she went shopping with her mum and that they had a KEY-CUTTING BIT and that she used her

pocket money to get a new key made.

That's when Jodi took a DEEP BREATH and said, "Maisie, where do you keep the spare key?" And she said it REALLY GENTLY and I knew that she was doing that because she knew Maisie was feeling

GUILTY

and also to make sure Maisie didn't faint before she got a chance to tell us where she kept the spare key.

And that's when Maisie closed her eyes and I thought she'd fainted again! But then she whispered, "I sellotaped it to the back of the photo frame on the wall outside the door."

Jodi LEAPED up and rushed outside and we all ran after her.

But when she took the frame off the wall and turned it around the SELLOTAPE was still there.

But the key was

GONE.

Before anyone could stop her, Jodi RAN out into the playground.

So we all ran after her.

And that's when we heard her shout, "It was you!"

And we rushed over and saw that Jodi was standing in front of the new girl, Jessi, and

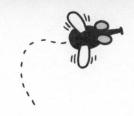

she was waving THE HAIR in her FACE.

We ran over and Jessi said, "EWW! Get your hair out my FACE!"

And Jodi said, "It's not my hair. It's YOURS. You left it in OUR DEN."

That's when the Jessi got a REALLY WEIRD look.

And then she laughed a bit and said, "I don't even know what you're talking about. What DEN? And how do you know it's my hair?"

And Jodi said, "Because I had the longest hair in the school until YOU came here. And it's longer than mine. So it MUST be yours."

And then Maisie said, "And we know you took the spare key. We've got your FINGERPRINTS. And we're going to give them to the POLICE."

And I was completely

SHOCKED

because I didn't expect Maisie to speak up to the new pupils like that! And I DEFINITELY didn't expect her to tell a LIE about us having their FINGERPRINTS!

The girl didn't say anything for a while after that.

And then eventually she smiled a

REALLY CREEPY

smile and said, "No need to involve the authorities. I just got a bit lost when I was looking for something, that's all." And she put out her hand for Maisie to shake and said, "Let's be friends."

But then, all of a sudden, the bell went and Jessi said, "Oh! Better run! Don't want to get told off!"

And then she ran away before any of us had a chance to say anything back.

We all stood in SHOCK for a moment because she had just ADMITTED to being in The Den!

Then Zach said, "She's obviously lying about why she was there. She must have gone LOOKING for a spare key and found one."

And we all nodded loads.

But then Miss Jones shouted for everyone to hurry up so we ran across the playground and into the school.

But when we were walking into class with everyone else, I noticed something. Jessi wasn't there. And neither were the others who sat at the table with her.

That's when I started to get a

REALLY WEIRD FEELING.

So I grabbed Jodi and Zach and said, "Stop. Something's not right."

And they STARED at me.

And that's when I said, "We need to go. Follow me."

And I ran.

INTRUDERS!

I ran all the way to The Den.

The door was shut when we got there and Zach went to get the key out of his bag but I put my hand on his arm and whispered, "I don't think we need it."

That's when Jodi GASPED and her eyes

went **WIDE**, and I reached out and turned the door handle and the door opened (even though we had locked it!).

And that's when we **ALL** gasped.

Because The Den was full of **ST BALTHAZAR'S** pupils.

Nobody said a WORD.

We just stood there staring at THEM and they stood there staring at US.

And then eventually Jodi said, "What are you all doing in OUR den?!"

And Jessi SMILED and said, "Who says it's YOUR den?! Maybe it's OUR den. We have a KEY, see?"

And then Jessi held the stolen key up and DANGLED it in front of Jodi's FACE.

I thought Jodi was going to

But she didn't. She just stood there STARING at Jessi with her arms crossed. But she didn't say another WORD.

Then Zavier said, "Jessi, we should go before Miss Veil gets annoyed."

And Jessi nodded and started to walk out.

Then she turned to Jodi and said, "Lock the door on your way out, please!"

And as soon as they were gone, Jodi SLAMMED the door behind them and rushed over and pulled up the loose floorboard.

My heart was POUNDING because I couldn't BELIEVE that we'd found them in OUR den and that they were trying to say that it was **THEIR** den now!

Maisie's eyes had gone all swirly and Zach was holding on to her **TIGHT** so that she didn't fall over.

Then Zach said, "So they obviously **DON'T** want to be friends. They were lying to us."

Then, all of a sudden, Jodi **SCREAMED**.

And that's when we saw that she was holding the loose floorboard in her hand and that her hand was **SHAKING**.

And she looked up at us with a **REALLY** worried look on her face and said, "They found our secret hiding place. They've got our **MEETING NOTEBOOK**."

Zach GASPED and Maisie slid down his leg and on to the ground.

Jodi stood up and she looked a bit like her FACE was shaking now too.

And then she said, "They know ... EVERYTHING."

When we got back to class, **BOTH** of our teachers had **GONE** so Jodi went **RIGHT** up to Jessi and said, "You'd better give it back. Now."

And Jessi stood up and said, "Is that a **THREAT**, Jodi?"

So that's when Jodi said, "No. It's not. It's **YOUR SCHOOL** that makes **THREATS**, remember? And it's **YOUR SCHOOL** that steals things. Not us."

That's when Zavier said, "We don't know what you're talking about."

And that made me **REALLY** annoyed

because they obviously DID know what we were talking about!

So I stepped forward and said, "I think you DO know, Zavier. You stole our notebook! You're

SPYING

on us! You're up to something! And we're going to find out WHAT because we ALWAYS do!"

And that's when Zavier stopped smiling and so did Jessi.

And I knew that it was because they knew

that **WE** knew they were up to something and that we were

SERIOUS

about finding out what it was and that we obviously weren't going to give up.

Then Jodi said, "That's right. We're **ON** to you! You won't get away with it."

Then, all of a sudden, Jessi said, "And what exactly do you think we're up to?"

And that's when Jodi stepped **REALLY CLOSE** to Jessi.

And then she said, "I think you're trying to

take over our SCHOOL."

And Jessi SMILED and stepped even CLOSER to Jodi so that their NOSES were almost TOUCHING.

And then she said, "This isn't YOUR school any more."

And we all

GASPED.

But then Miss Jones and Miss Veil BOTH rushed into the class at the same time and said, "Sorry! We're here! We had a meeting!"

And then Jessi looked at us and smiled

fakely and whispered, "I guess we'll just have to see who wins on Friday..."

We had

NO IDEA

what was happening on Friday but we knew
that whatever it was, we had to **WIN**.

I put my hand up and said that I was going to ask Miss Jones but then Jodi took my hand and PINNED IT to the table and said, "NO. That will make us look WEAK."

And then she said that we had to PRETEND that we KNEW what was happening on Friday (even though we didn't) because it was OUR school and that we couldn't let them think that THEY knew more about what was going on at OUR school than WE did.

And that's when Maisie said, "But they do! They knew about the secret classrooms before Miss Jones even told us!"

Jodi nodded REALLY SLOWLY when Maisie said that. And she made her EYES go really thin and almost shut them and I knew that she was THINKING.

Then Zach whispered, "I know! Maybe they're PSYCHIC and can tell the future!"

And then Jodi's eyes went even MORE THIN and she rubbed her CHIN a bit and said, "Or they're

SPYING

on the WHOLE SCHOOL. Including the teachers and probably even the HEAD TEACHER!"

And we all

because that was SERIOUS.

Then, all of a sudden, the classroom door FLEW open and a pupil I've never seen before ran in and yelled, "RATS! RATS EVERYWHERE! GET OUT!"

And everyone started SCREAMING.

Everyone had to stay in the lunch hall until

PEST CONTROL

had left. And then we all got given a **LETTER** and were told to put it in our bags and give it to our parents or carers to open and that we were **NOT** to open it first.

So we all opened our letters and that's when we

GASPED

because it said that there had been a

"SUSPECTED
RAT SIGHTING"

in the school and that PEST CONTROL
had attended and that the situation was

UNDER CONTROL.

That's when Jodi said, "Who was it who
saw the rat?"

And Zavier overheard us and said,
"It was us. We saw TWO actually."

And Jodi said, "Where?"

And that's when Jessi said, "We saw them in the classroom. It's disgusting!"

I couldn't believe it so that's when I said, "OUR classroom?!"

Because I was totally

    FREAKED OUT

that there were RATS in our classroom!

Then Jessi said, "It's terrible, isn't it? Disgusting!"

And then Jessi looked RIGHT at Maisie and said, "What if one of us gets BITTEN?"

And there was SOMETHING about the way Jessi looked at MAISIE when she said it that told me she was trying to scare her!

And it worked. Because Maisie fainted INSTANTLY and Jessi started shouting, "OH MY GOODNESS! HELP! HELP! I THINK SHE WAS BITTEN BY A RAT!"

And that's when EVERYONE started

SCREAMING and

RUNNING ABOUT

and me and Jodi and Zach actually had to

PULL Maisie up off the ground really quickly
so that she didn't get TRAMPLED.

Operation Straight Hair!

The next day, ALL the NEW PUPILS were wearing WELLIES to school with their trousers tucked in so that the RATS couldn't climb up their LEGS.

And Jessi and Zavier WOULDN'T stop talking about it and asked Miss Jones

LOADS of questions!

Then at break we overheard Mika telling loads of people that the school should be **SHUT DOWN** because it was **UNSAFE** and **RIDDLED WITH RATS**.

I was starting to

because I didn't want our school to get **SHUT DOWN** because I had

which school we would have to go to if that happened, and I didn't want us to all get split up and sent to different schools!

But that's when Jodi said, "Don't worry. I will

let that happen."

And there was something about the WAY she said it and her FACE and her EYES that made me feel better because Jodi is a VERY determined person and if she says she is going to do something then she always does it. Like the time she wanted to join the boys' football team and she DID.

So anyway, that's when Jodi whispered, "Did any of you see a rat in our classroom?"

And we all said no.

And then Jodi said, "EXACTLY. But somehow Jessi and the others have seen SIX?"

And then she NARROWED her eyes and STARED over at where Mika was telling a big group of pupils about

THE RATS.

And I looked and saw that she was waving her arms **ALL OVER** the place and that Jessi was doing a fake **BITING THING** with her mouth and that everyone looked

SHOCKED.

Then Zach gasped and looked at Jodi and said, "You think they're making it up!"

And Jodi nodded and said, "I do. I think they **WANT** everyone to believe that there are rats in the classroom."

So that's when I asked why they would do that because it didn't make any sense.

But Jodi just shook her head and said, "I don't know. We need to find out what they're up to."

And then she looked right at me and said, "I have a plan."

I thought that Jodi's plan was GREAT until she said that I was the one who had to go

Jodi said that she'd seen a SIGN saying that there was an ASSEMBLY tomorrow but that it was only for ST BALTHAZAR'S

pupils and that one of us needed to be there to find out what it was about and that that someone was ME.

I was

when Jodi said that because I didn't understand why she was saying that it needed to be ME and also because SHE usually volunteers to go on all the

DANGEROUS MISSIONS.

So I said that I thought **JODI** should be the one to go **UNDERCOVER** but Jodi said that Jessi would spot her a **MILE AWAY** because she is quite **TALL**, and also that I was the only one that could be

COMPLETELY TRANSFORMED.

I didn't really know what Jodi meant about me being

TRANSFORMED

but when we got to Jodi's house that night I knew that it had something to do with my HAIR because Jodi had set up a HAIRDRESSING CHAIR in the living room.

Then Jodi's mum said that she was going to help Jodi do the

TRANSFORMATION

because Jodi's mum used to work in a hairdresser's and now she's a FULLY TRAINED DOG GROOMER.

I was a bit nervous because I didn't know WHAT they were going to do.

But then Jodi's mum got out HAIR STRAIGHTENERS and said that she was going to STRAIGHTEN my hair so that it wasn't

WILD

any more and that it would make me look like a NEW PERSON.

I was a bit nervous because I've never had my hair straightened before and I was worried that it was going to HURT. But Jodi's mum said that it wouldn't and that it would actually be very RELAXING.

So I sat down and Jodi's mum started straightening my hair. But it definitely WASN'T relaxing because she kept getting the brush stuck and saying that my hair was HARD WORK and that she was

SWEATING.

Then she went and got ANOTHER pair of straighteners and told Jodi to help her so that we weren't there "ALL NIGHT".

So I just sat there while Jodi and her mum straightened my hair and Zach and Maisie had to help by holding up bits of it so that

Jodi's mum could get the underneath bits because I have a

LOT of hair.

Then when it was eventually finished, Jodi's mum drank a WHOLE BOTTLE OF WATER in ONE GO without taking a breath. And then she wiped the SWEAT off her forehead and said that doing my hair had been worse than the time she'd had to groom a

MATTED POODLE.

That's when I realised that **EVERYONE** was staring at me. Especially Jodi.

Then Jodi put the mirror in front of me and told me to look and that's when I realised why everyone was staring so much and why they all had **SHOCKED LOOKS** on their faces.

They were staring at me because I looked like a completely DIFFERENT PERSON.

Zach kept saying, "I can't believe it's YOU. I can't believe it's YOU!"

And that's when I actually burst out laughing and starting swishing my hair about because I couldn't believe how LONG and FLOATY it was!

I looked at Jodi and she was smiling LOADS and I knew that it was because her plan was working.

So that's when I had an idea, so I said, "Jodi, do you still have your old glasses?"

(Because Jodi wears CONTACT LENSES

now but she used to wear glasses.)

And Jodi RAN to get them and I put them on and looked at everyone.

And Jodi smiled a HUGE smile and said,

"PERFECT."

Undercover

The next day, we waited until the last group of **NEW PUPILS** had walked into the assembly hall and then Jodi said, "**GO!**" and I snuck in behind them and sat at the **VERY BACK** of the hall next to the **BIG PLANT** like we'd agreed.

I felt a bit like I was going to be SICK and it wasn't just because the glasses were making me DIZZY – it was because I was

UNDERCOVER,

pretending to be a St Balthazar's pupil!

I was even wearing a St Balthazar's BLAZER that Maisie had got in the LOST AND FOUND at school.

I put as MUCH of my hair in front of my face as I could so people couldn't see me properly and waited for the assembly to start.

I had

what the assembly was about because the poster on the notice board didn't say. It just said, "9 A.M. SHARP!"

But then, all of a sudden, MISS VEIL came on stage and said loads of stuff in some sort of WEIRD LANGUAGE.

And everyone stood up and started CHANTING really weird words over and over again, and one of them was "RATTUS".

So I stood up too because I was

UNDERCOVER. But I had to hold on to the chair in front of me because my LEGS were SHAKING because of all the CHANTING.

But then all of a sudden MR GRAVES walked on stage and the chanting STOPPED and Miss Veil started speaking in ENGLISH and everyone sat down and pretended like they hadn't just been doing the CHANTING, and I knew that it was because Mr Graves had CAUGHT THEM.

But then as soon as Mr Graves walked off stage MISS VEIL started CHANTING AGAIN and I heard the word

"RATTUS"

over and over again!

I felt like I was going to

FAINT

but somehow I managed to stay CONSCIOUS until every single person had left the assembly hall.

Then when everyone was gone I tried to sneak out from behind the big plant where I'd been hiding but I COULDN'T MOVE.

I started to panic because I thought that maybe the new pupils had SPOTTED me and that the chanting had cast a SPELL on me or something!

But then I realised that it was because I was SCARED and that my legs had gone into SHOCK.

So that's when I shouted, "HELP!" and

Jodi and the others came rushing in and I explained what was going on and Jodi said that I needed to

and that my body was holding on to TRAUMA and that whatever I'd WITNESSED was obviously REALLY BAD and that it had SCARED MY BODY and that I needed to

Then Jodi took off my glasses and started to sing a LULLABY to me, but that didn't help because Jodi doesn't have a very relaxing voice and it sounded a bit CREEPY and definitely NOT relaxing, so I had to ask her to stop.

And Zach started laughing because he knew that I'd asked her to stop because it sounded creepy and that made ME laugh a bit too, even though I DEFINITELY didn't feel like laughing because my legs weren't working!

But the laughing made me feel better and relaxed me a bit and I started to be able to

move my legs.

Then Jodi tried to say that she sang weird on purpose but none of us believed her because she'd looked like she was trying really hard to sing WELL like she does when we go to the church at the end of the street at Christmas.

So anyway, that's when Jodi said, "Tell us. Tell us everything!"

And then she explained that they couldn't hear anything from outside and that St Balthazar's must have had the doors SOUNDPROOFED before the assembly.

So then I took a deep breath and said, "It's bad. Like,

REALLY bad."

And that's when Maisie grabbed hold of the big plant TIGHT and said, "No, no, no, no!"

But Jodi said, "Go on. Were they talking about school dinners? Or taking over the school?"

And I shook my head and said, "No. It was WORSE. They were CHANTING!"

And Maisie made a really loud squeaking noise for ages and Jodi leaned in close and said, "Izzy. You need to tell us EXACTLY what they said."

And that's when I shook my head and said, "No."

And Jodi's EYES went wide.

And then I said, "I wish I could. But I can't."

And Zach said, "What do you mean you can't?!"

That's when I looked at Zach and said, "I can't because they weren't speaking in English. They were chanting in a weird language that I've never heard before!"

And Zach said, "Are you sure it wasn't French?"

But I shook my head because **WE** do French at our school and I definitely hadn't heard anything like **THAT** before.

Then Jodi said, "Are you sure, Izzy? I mean, you're not that good at French."

And I nodded that I was sure.

And Zach said, "How?"

And I said, "Because they were chanting the same

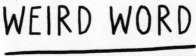

WEIRD WORD

loads and I've never heard it before."

And Jodi's eyes went EVEN WIDER and she said, "What was the word?"

And I took a deep breath and said, "RATTUS."

And that's when Maisie grabbed the BIG PLANT and HUGGED IT TIGHT and it started shaking all OVER the place and loads of LEAVES fell off on to the floor.

It Was THEM!

It was **IMPOSSIBLE** to get Maisie to let go of the **BIG PLANT** because her **NAILS** were **BURIED** deep into the **TRUNK**.

And in the end we actually had to carry Maisie **AND** the plant **AND** the pot all the way to The Den.

When we got there, Maisie said, "Ribena, Twix, blanket ... ALL!"

And we GASPED and looked at each other because Maisie has never ASKED for EVERYTHING all at once like that before.

That's when Zach said, "She needs the FULL WORKS. This must be BAD."

So me and Zach fed Maisie Ribena through a straw and Jodi gently removed Maisie's fingernails from the plant one by one until the plant was free.

Then Jodi put the EXTRA PAIR OF SOCKS that we keep in The Den on Maisie's feet because they get VERY COLD when she's scared and Jodi saw a programme that said you need to keep the **BLOOD MOVING** when you get a shock.

That's when Zach said that The Den looked quite nice with a big plant in it and that maybe we should bring some more stuff from home to make it look nice.

And I was a bit

that Zach was talking about DECORATING

when Maisie was in the middle of a

TRAUMATIC EXPERIENCE,

so I gave him a look.

But then he gave me a look BACK and said, "Maybe another bookcase. This place would look great with even more books in it, don't you think, Maisie?"

And that's when I realised that he was trying to take Maisie's mind off whatever

TRAUMATIC EXPERIENCE

she'd had in the assembly hall.

I didn't think it was going to work but then Maisie lifted up her little arm and pointed to the wall next to the sink and said, "There. A bookcase would look good there."

And I smiled because even though she was still lying down with her eyes shut TIGHT, she couldn't help herself because she really loves books.

So we waited until Maisie had stopped drinking Ribena and had eaten her first finger of Twix and then Jodi said, "Tell us why you freaked out back there, Maisie. It's OK."

And Maisie shook her head and said NO, and that it WASN'T OK, and that it probably wouldn't ever be OK ever again.

And then she looked at me RIGHT in the eyes and whispered, "I know what 'RATTUS' means!"

And we all GASPED because we couldn't believe Maisie knew the secret language the St Balthazar's pupils had been chanting!

I started to feel LIGHT-HEADED so

I grabbed Maisie's other TWIX finger and started to eat it because I knew that whatever she said next wasn't going to be GOOD because Maisie had been so scared she'd hugged a PLANT!

And that's when Maisie said, "It means 'RAT' in LATIN."

And Zach jumped up and yelled,

"I KNEW IT. I KNEW IT WAS GOING TO MEAN 'RAT' IN LATIN!"

And Jodi said, "Maisie, are you sure?"

And Maisie said that she was sure and that she didn't know a LOT of Latin words but that she knew that one and it meant "RAT".

And Jodi said, "It was THEM. They're SUMMONING the rats here with their secret-society chanting!"

That's when Zach said, "But why would they do that?"

And Jodi stood up and put her hands on her hips and said, "THAT'S what we need to find out." And then she said, "We need to learn LATIN ASAP so we can stop whatever they're going to do next!"

The Library Thieves

So it turns out that it's IMPOSSIBLE to learn Latin.

And I know that I'm DEFINITELY not the only person who thinks so because Maisie told us that LATIN is now actually A DEAD LANGUAGE, which means that it's not even

USED anywhere by anyone any more! And I wasn't surprised to hear that because it's REALLY HARD.

So anyway, we went to the school library at break and asked for a LATIN DICTIONARY and Jodi WHISPERED when she asked Miss Bottery for it because we didn't want any of the NEW PUPILS to overhear us and know that we were ON TO THEM.

Jodi hid the dictionary in her bag and then we snuck over to our favourite seats that are hidden behind the biggest bookcase.

Zach took one of the books off the shelf so we could peek through the gap and make

sure no one was LISTENING to us and then he said, "CLEAR," and Jodi nodded so we opened the dictionary.

Jodi said that we needed to learn as MANY of the Latin words as possible and that it would be good if one of us could become FLUENT ASAP, which meant that she wanted one of us to actually be able to speak FULL LATIN.

So we all looked at Maisie but she shook her head LOADS and said, "It's really hard! The head teacher at my old school made us do it every day when we were in Year One and I only learned a few words!"

And then Zach said, "Like 'Rattus'?"

And Maisie nodded and looked down at the ground and I didn't know why she did that but I thought it was probably because she was scared because "RATTUS" means "RATS" and she was scared in case there were RATS running near her feet.

So that's when I said that we didn't need to become FLUENT in Latin and that all we needed was the dictionary so that we could look up any words we OVERHEARD the new pupils saying.

But when we took the book up to the librarian's desk, Miss Bottery said, "You can't

take the dictionaries out, I'm afraid. We need to keep them in the library in case someone needs them. But you're welcome to come in and use it any time."

Then, all of a sudden, there was a CRASHING NOISE at the other side of the library and someone shouted, "SORRY!" and Miss Bottery went rushing over to see what the crash had been about.

And THAT'S when Jodi unzipped her bag and slipped the LATIN DICTIONARY inside, and Maisie GASPED and said, "Jodi. We can't. That's STEALING."

But Jodi just zipped her bag up TIGHT

and said, "We don't have a choice. We have to save our school. Let's go!"

I could hardly concentrate in class because of the STOLEN DICTIONARY in Jodi's bag. I kept imagining that it was

GLOWING RED

because it was STOLEN, and even though that OBVIOUSLY wouldn't happen, I kept having to CHECK because I was PANICKING. And EVERY time Miss Jones or Miss Veil passed by I held my breath.

But Maisie was

FREAKING
OUT MUCH WORSE

than I was. She kept TUGGING at Jodi's arm and saying, "We need to take it back! We're THIEVES!"

But Jodi said that we needed to keep it CLOSE in case we overheard the new pupils use another LATIN WORD so that we could ACT QUICKLY. And that we WEREN'T thieves because we were going to give it back once we'd saved the school.

Then, all of a sudden, the classroom door

BURST open and I actually SCREAMED a bit because I thought it was the POLICE come to ARREST US.

But it wasn't the police. It was Mr Graves the head teacher and he looked

MEGA WEIRD.

He looked at all of us and said, "Children, I would like to introduce you to—"

But then the door flew open AGAIN and a WOMAN came rushing in and all the St Balthazar's pupils GASPED and someone said, "It's Laser Linghams! She's here!"

x

208

I had **NO IDEA** who **LASER LINGHAMS** was, but then the woman said, "Children, I would like to introduce myself to those of you who I haven't had the pleasure of meeting yet."

But then before the woman could say anything else Mr Graves said, "Yes. I was just about to explain to our pupils and staff that—"

But then the woman started talking over Mr Graves again and said, "I'm Ms Linghams, your head teacher."

And we all GASPED and Miss Jones SQUEAKED and Mr Graves said, "I'M the head teacher!"

And that's when Ms Linghams turned and gave him the most TERRIFYING LOOK I have EVER seen and that's when I realised why her pupils called her LASER LINGHAMS.

Mr Graves GULPED a bit and then Laser Linghams SMILED a CREEPY SMILE and said, "We'll just have to wait until FRIDAY to see about that!"

I GASPED and so did Jodi because something

BIG

was happening on Friday and it looked like it had to do with who was going to be the HEAD TEACHER of our school!

"It's On My CHIPS!"

We were the last class to arrive at lunch that day because Mr Graves and Laser Linghams wouldn't stop ARGUING in front of us about who the head teacher was, even though the bell had gone!

And by the time we got to the dining hall it

was CHAOS. Zach's mouth fell WIDE OPEN and Jodi said, "OH. MY. GOSH."

There was food ALL OVER the floor and everyone was SCREAMING and running around.

We had

NO IDEA

what was going on.

Then one of the Year 6s shouted, "IT'S ON MY CHIPS!"

And then she THREW her plate of chips against the wall and the plate smashed and

the chips went flying EVERYWHERE.

And then someone at the OPPOSITE end of the dining hall screamed,

"WATCH OUT! THEY CAN FLY! ARRGHHH!!"

I looked around to see what the teachers were doing but I couldn't actually SEE any of them because there were FLYING INSECTS everywhere!

I looked over at the dinner ladies and they were all waving their ICE-CREAM SCOOPS around in the air and SLAMMING them

against the counter, trying to **KILL** the insects.

Then someone screamed,

"THERE ARE
THOUSANDS OF THEM!"

And one of the Year 6s yelled, "They're in the pies!

THEY'RE FLY PIES!"

EVERYONE was EVACUATED from the dining hall and back to class. And when we got there NO ONE would calm down about the thousands of FLYING INSECTS, even when Miss Jones told us it had only been a few FLIES and that PEST CONTROL were on their way again.

But everyone was asking why they had been INSIDE the food! And Miss Jones just shook her head and said that she didn't know but that it was all being taken care of and that there was nothing to worry about.

That's when I whispered to Jodi, "Do you think THEY did this?"

And Jodi nodded.

Then the St Balthazar's pupils actually stood up and started saying that it had been like THE PLAGUE and that WHO KNOWS what other HORRIBLE THINGS were in the CUPBOARDS and SINK in the school kitchen and that the FRIDGE was probably

TOXIC.

Then they said that they thought the school was UNSAFE and UNHYGENIC and that they should all be sent home for HEALTH AND SAFETY REASONS.

That's when everyone started SHOUTING OUT at Miss Jones and saying that they FELT SICK and POISONED and that they needed to go and see the NURSE.

But then Miss Veil and the OFFICE LADIES turned up with PACKED LUNCHES and everyone calmed down right away.

But the packed lunches weren't like NORMAL packed lunches that we usually get when we're going on a SCHOOL TRIP and when I opened mine I actually

GASPED

because it was prawns on TOAST! And I HATE prawns!

Jodi got a big box of TOFU. And Zach got half a Peking duck (which he loved, and he said that he was going to have that for his packed lunch from now on).

Jodi was STARING at Jessi and the other St Balthazar's pupils while she ate her tofu. And then when she finished she said, "We could have stopped the

FLY PIE ATTACK

if we'd known what they were planning.

They're up to something and we need to BE ONE STEP AHEAD. I think they're trying to replace OUR dinner ladies with THEIR dinner ladies as part of their takeover. It's the only explanation. We need to stop them!"

That's when I said that maybe it wouldn't be the WORST thing in the world if they replaced our dinner ladies because then maybe we wouldn't have to eat the poisonous shepherd's pie all the time!

But Jodi said, "NO WAY. First they steal our TABLE, then they bring in their TEACHERS when we've already got our own, and try to replace our DINNER LADIES and now this

LASER-LINGHAMS

PERSON

is saying she's the new head teacher! We have to do something before they REPLACE US and take over the whole school and we have to go to another school!"

That's when Maisie put her hand up and asked to go the toilet and Miss Jones gave her a

TOILET PASS.

And then JUST before Maisie walked out of the door she turned and looked RIGHT at me and WINKED.

Me and Jodi both GASPED.

And then Jodi said, "That's was a SIGNAL!"

Jodi said that I should wait for a minute before putting my hand up so it didn't look SUSPICIOUS.

So I nodded and waited EXACTLY sixty seconds, and I know

that it was sixty seconds because I was counting in my head the whole time and it felt like AGES!

Then I put my hand up and asked if I could go to the toilet and as SOON as the classroom door shut behind me I RAN all the way to The Den because I knew that that was where Maisie would be and I was right!

Maisie GRABBED me and gave me a HUGE HUG and then she looked RIGHT at me and said, "I need to tell you something. I can't keep it a secret any more."

And I just nodded because I have never SEEN Maisie act so weird before.

And then she said, "I'm one of them."

I had

what she meant, and I was just about to ask

her if she needed to lie down when she said,

"I'm from St Balthazar's. I'm so sorry."

NO WAY, MAISIE!

I didn't say ANYTHING for AGES.

I just stood there STARING at Maisie, trying to understand what she was saying to me!

Then Maisie said, "Izzy, did you hear what I said?"

And I nodded.

And Maisie nodded too and said, "I'm sorry I didn't tell you. I couldn't."

And then, all of a sudden, JODI came BURSTING into The Den and she had a TOILET PASS in her hand and she said, "WHAT? WHAT HAPPENED? WHY DID YOU GUYS COME HERE? DID YOU FIND OUT SOMETHING ABOUT THE NEW PUPILS AND THE FLY PIES?"

I looked at Maisie and she looked

TERRIFIED

and Jodi said, "What? WHAT?!"

And then Zach appeared and I said I thought that was WEIRD because there was

NO WAY

Miss Jones would give the FOUR of us TOILET PASSES at the same time because she knows that we're BEST FRIENDS.

Then Zach smiled and said, "We asked Miss Veil! She doesn't even know who we are so she let us go at the same time!"

And that's when Maisie GRABBED Jodi and Zach and PULLED them towards her

and said, "Please sit down."

And I could just TELL by the look on both Jodi's and Zach's FACES that they were SHOCKED at the way Maisie was BEING and SPEAKING because usually she is SUPER QUIET and shy and SCARED, but she wasn't being ANY of those things!

Jodi STARED at me and then raised her eyebrows a bit, which meant that she was asking me if Maisie was OK. But I just looked down at the ground and didn't reply with my eyes OR eyebrows because Maisie was NOT OK.

Because she was ONE OF THEM. And

that meant that she was probably a

that had been sent here on an

UNDERCOVER MISSION

and that we'd been

I looked at Maisie but she didn't say anything. She just looked back at me and **NODDED**, and that's when I realised that she'd asked me to come to The Den with her because she wanted to tell me her secret and then she wanted **ME** to be the one to tell everyone else because she was probably too scared.

So that's when I took a deep breath and said, "Maisie isn't who we think she is."

And Jodi's **EYES** went wide and Zach said, "What do you mean?"

And I couldn't actually **BELIEVE** that I was saying what I was saying but I **HAD** to and so that's when I said, "She's one of them!"

And Zach looked at Maisie and Jodi and me and then back at Maisie and said, "One of who?"

Jodi looked JUST as confused as Zach did and I knew that it was because

would suspect Maisie of being a

which is obviously why she was the best

person EVER to be sent here from St Balzathar's to spy on us!

And that's when I said, "She's from St Balthazar's."

And Jodi GASPED and Zach said, "No."

And Maisie nodded that I was telling the truth and Zach GULPED.

And then I said, "She was sent here to spy on us. She's UNDERCOVER."

And then I looked down at my shoes because I felt like I was going to start CRYING because saying it out loud was TOO MUCH because I LOVED Maisie and she was one of my best friends and I couldn't believe that she wasn't really our friend.

And that's when Maisie said, "WHAT? NO. NO. NO. NO!"

I whipped my head round to see Maisie's face and she looked PANICKED, and that's when she said, "Yes. I'm from St Balthazar's but I'm not a spy! I'm not undercover!"

My head was **SPINNING** because I couldn't understand what she was saying.

But then Jodi said, "Maisie, are you a spy for our arch-enemy? If I ask you directly and look into your eyes, you have to tell me the truth because that's the **LAW** under the

⭐ **OFFICIAL SECRETS** ⭐
ACT OF THE UNITED KINGDOM."

And then she **STARED AT MAISIE** and waited for her response.

And that's when Maisie **STARED BACK** and said, "**NO**. I'm not a **SPY**. But I **AM** a

St Balthazar's pupil."

Zach stood up and shook his head really fast as if he was trying to clear his BRAIN, and then he said, "I don't understand. WHAT?!"

And that's when Maisie said that she had gone to St Balthazar's in Year 1 and a bit of Year 2 before she moved to OUR school and that she never told us because she didn't want us to HATE HER because she knew about the INCIDENT and she didn't want us to think that she was a THIEF because she didn't know ANYTHING about the trophy.

So that's when I said, "But you said that

you didn't know about the trophy and the incident!"

And Maisie looked down at the ground and said, "I know. I was worried that you were all going to find out who I REALLY was and that you wouldn't want to be friends with me any more. So I lied. I even changed the way I LOOKED so people wouldn't know who I was. I didn't want anyone here to find out I was one of them. But I am. And I'm sorry."

And that's when Zach said, "That's how you knew the Latin word 'Rattus', isn't it? You did Latin at St Balthazar's?"

And Maisie nodded.

And then Zach said, "You know Jessi and the rest of them, don't you? And that was your old blazer too, wasn't it? You didn't find it in the Lost and Found?"

And Maisie nodded again.

And then she said, "I'm sorry for lying to you. But I'm not one of them now, I promise. But I could be…"

I looked at Maisie and said, "What?"

Jodi's eyes went wide because she obviously knew what Maisie meant.

And that's when Maisie said, "I want to make it up to you all. I'm sorry for lying and not telling you who I really was."

And that's when I felt like I was going to start CRYING again, so I said, "Maisie, you don't have to make it up to us. I understand why you didn't tell us. And I believe you that you're not like them and that you didn't steal the trophy. You're our friend and you're one of US now."

And then Zach said, "Yes. You're one of us."

And Jodi got up and gave Maisie a HUGE HUG, and I was a bit shocked because Jodi doesn't do that very often.

And then Maisie smiled and said, "Thank you. But I'd still like to make up for lying and

I want to help save our school."

And then Jodi said, "What do you mean?"

And Maisie said, "I'm going to go undercover. DEEP undercover."

And I

GASPED.

We've Lost Maisie

The next morning, Maisie walked **RIGHT** up to Jessi and the others and started talking. At first they just **LOOKED** at her. But then she took her **BLAZER** out of her bag and put it on and, all of a sudden, they **GASPED** and **HUGGED** her and said, "**MAISIE MILLER!**

It's YOU!"

Then at break Maisie stayed with Jessi and the rest of them and she even sat with them at dinners!

It felt SO WEIRD seeing Maisie with them and her not being with us, but I knew that it was only for ONE DAY until she found out what they were PLANNING and why they had done the

FLY PIE.

But then the next day Maisie sat next to Jessi in class AGAIN and at break she didn't meet us in The Den like she was supposed to and that's when Jodi said, "I was worried this might happen."

And I said, "WHAT?" because if Jodi was worried, then I was worried too.

And that's when Jodi said, "I think she's gone

TOO DEEP UNDERCOVER."

I looked at Zach and he looked PALE, and then Jodi said, "I think we might have lost her."

That afternoon I watched Maisie in PE and she was acting really differently and laughing loads and JUMPING and I have never seen her jump even ONCE.

That's when Zach said that he thought I

should go up to her and SHAKE HER so that she wasn't BRAINWASHED any more.

But Jodi said, "No. Let's just wait. Time will tell!"

And that's when Maisie started walking towards us REALLY FAST and then she walked RIGHT past us and she didn't even LOOK at us!

She just FLICKED her hair and I have NEVER seen Maisie flick her hair.

I looked down because I felt terrible and THAT'S when I saw it.

There was a piece of scrunched-up paper at my feet.

I looked over at Maisie and she looked over her shoulder at me and WINKED, and that's when I gasped and grabbed the paper and opened it and it said,

"THEY'RE PLANNING SOMETHING BIG. MEET ME IN THE DEN."

The NOT Fun Day!

Maisie found out LOADS when she was undercover.

She said that she'd had to be CAREFUL so they didn't suspect her, but that she was SURE it was them who'd planted all the FLIES in the FLY PIE because she'd found a DOODLE of a fly in Zavier's PERSONAL NOTEBOOK and a Latin word underneath.

Maisie said that she'd MEMORISED the word and Jodi patted her on the back and said that that was an "EXCELLENT" thing to have done and that writing it down would have been

TOO RISKY

while she was DEEP UNDERCOVER, and Maisie nodded and smiled and I could tell that she was enjoying being a spy a little bit.

So that's when Maisie said that the word

was "MUSCA" and Jodi flicked through the Latin dictionary and then looked up at us and said, "FLY."

And Zach said, "So it WAS them! But why?!"

Maisie said that she didn't know but that she'd overheard Jessi talking about a PLAN and she seemed

REALLY SERIOUS

about it and that she kept hearing her say the same word to Zavier a LOT. And Maisie had memorised that one too.

Then she opened her eyes wide and said, "LACTRODACTAL."

But we couldn't find it in the dictionary.

Zach said that he thought that it must have something to do with DINOSAURS because it sounded like PTERODACTYL.

Then, all of a sudden, there was a KNOCK at the The Den door and Jodi said, "Shhh!"

So we all went silent and didn't say anything.

And then a voice outside said, "It's Jessi. I thought you might want to see this hot off the press!"

And then she slipped an A4 poster under

the door and laughed and we heard her running away.

Jodi **GRABBED** the poster and then she read it and turned it round for us to see and it said:

⭐ **SPECIAL ANNOUNCEMENT!** ⭐
⭐ **THERE WILL BE A WHOLE** ⭐
⭐ **SCHOOL FUN DAY THIS FRIDAY** ⭐
LET THE FUN AND GAMES BEGIN!

That's when I gasped because we'd forgotten **ALL** about the thing Jessi had said about finding something out on

FRIDAY because of the

FLY PIE

and the UNDERCOVER STUFF and almost losing Maisie to the OTHER SIDE.

That's when Zach gulped and said, "Why do I get the feeling that this isn't going to be very FUN at all!"

Zach was right. There was NOTHING fun about the FUN DAY.

ALL the teachers were ACTING WEIRD and doing loads of STRETCHES and

Mr Beattie said he'd only been drinking **VEGGIE JUICE** for **THREE DAYS** and that his body was **READY**.

We didn't really know what he was getting ready for because Miss Jones had said that it was a **FUN DAY** to help us all get to know one another **BETTER** and to make our school **ONE BIG HAPPY FAMILY**.

But the teachers didn't look very happy at ALL and Mr Graves even looked a bit like he was going to be SICK.

Then we overheard Mr Killington say, "This is WAR."

And Laser Linghams SCREAMED into a megaphone, "Let the games begin!"

Everyone GASPED and covered their ears and we watched as all the teachers started to RUN.

That's when Zach said, "Oh no. I know what's happening! I saw this on TV!"

We all turned to stare at Zach and he said that he'd watched a film with his mum and that it was all about these people FIGHTING AGAINST each other for FOOD and WATER and their LIVES.

I looked at Jodi and she looked at me and then we BOTH looked at Miss Jones, and THAT'S when we realised what was happening.

And Jodi said, "They're fighting for their JOBS. They're fighting to STAY HERE!"

That's when Jessi's voice came out of NOWHERE and she said, "YUP!"

We all gasped and turned round to see Jessi and Zavier standing RIGHT behind us and they were both smiling REALLY

CREEPY SMILES.

And then Jessi said, "May the best school win!"

⭐

Things got completely out of hand after that.

It started with a SACK RACE. ALL the teachers were fighting over the BEST SACKS and Mr Beattie ended up with one that was so small that he had to CROUCH DOWN like a FROG just to fit in it.

Mr Graves and Laser Linghams were PULLING at the megaphone because they EACH wanted to be the one who shouted, "GO!" into it.

But then Laser Linghams bent down and shouted "GO!" even though it was Mr Graves who was holding it, and all the teachers went

WILD.

Miss Veil was winning for AGES, but then Mr Killington JUMPED in front of her and she

SCREAMED

and started to jump even FASTER until they were NECK AND NECK, and then she PUSHED HIM OVER into the grass!

Mr Graves was shouting

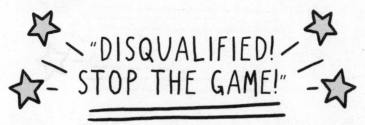

"DISQUALIFIED! STOP THE GAME!"

but the teachers weren't listening.

Then Miss Jones's sack RIPPED and she got SO ANGRY that she STOLE one of the new teachers' sacks and then jumped REALLY FAST all the way to the finishing line and won!

We went

when Miss Jones won and Mr Graves yelled

"WHOOP" into the megaphone.

But then Laser Linghams GRABBED it out of Mr Graves's hand and yelled,

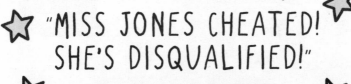

"MISS JONES CHEATED!
SHE'S DISQUALIFIED!"

But the teachers STILL weren't listening and Mr Beattie and Mrs Leppard had actually picked Miss Jones UP and they were carrying her around the playground, and she was WAVING her ARMS around, shouting, "WE ARE THE CHAMPIONS!"

Then they did a PASS THE BATON race. Mr Beattie ran SUPER FAST and he was WINNING until Laser Linghams COUGHED really loudly into the megaphone and Mr Beattie got a fright and DROPPED THE BATON.

And that's when he screamed,

"NOOOOOOOOOOOOOOOOOO!"

and bent over to pick it up and FAINTED! We RAN over and put Mr Beattie in the recovery position and I thought the race would STOP but it DIDN'T.

All the teachers just kept RUNNING PAST US with their BATONS, so we had to form a CIRCLE round Mr Beattie to keep him SAFE until the AMBULANCE got there. The PARAMEDICS looked

SHOCKED

when they arrived, and one of them asked us if we were OK, and we said that we were and that our teachers were just FIGHTING FOR THEIR JOBS, and the paramedics didn't say anything after that. They just gave Mr Beattie FLUIDS, and when he woke up he got told to eat a sandwich

ASAP

and that **NO ONE** could live on just **VEGGIE SHAKES** alone.

Then when the paramedics tried to get back in their ambulance and leave, Mr Graves said, "No. I think you'd better stay."

And Laser Linghams yelled,

"IT'S TIME FOR THE JAVELIN-THROWING CONTEST!"

And that's when we realised that the FUN DAY wasn't going to stop. Even though Mr Beattie had FAINTED and almost been TRAMPLED TO DEATH by the other teachers.

Then Zach asked if the PUPILS were going to get to take part because we hadn't been allowed to do ANYTHING yet!

But Mr Graves didn't answer because he was too busy trying to pull the CLIPBOARD out of Laser Linghams' HANDS.

Then Zach gulped REALLY LOUDLY and that's when we looked where he was looking and saw that the teachers were now

holding LONG POINTY JAVELINS.

And Laser Linghams screamed, "THROW THEM AS FAR AS YOU CAN!"

Maisie covered her eyes and Zach went very pale, and I looked at Jodi and she looked at me and I could tell that she was just as relieved as I was that the ambulance was still here!

Then Mr Beattie tried to get up off the little bed in the ambulance and take part in the JAVELIN CONTEST, but the paramedics pushed him back down and said, "Take it easy. You need to rest."

And that's when Mr Beattie yelled, "NEVER!"

And then he tried to JUMP out of the ambulance and fainted AGAIN.

That's when I spotted something that freaked me out, and I tugged on Jodi's sleeve and pointed, and she looked and said, "Oh."

And then she didn't say anything else after that. And that was probably because she had

NO IDEA

what to say because Miss Jones was bent down in the grass and she was rubbing her

FINGERS in the MUD and then putting the mud on her FACE.

That's when Zach GASPED and said that Miss Jones was making "WAR MARKS" on her face and that things were about to get WORSE.

My mouth actually DROPPED WIDE OPEN when Zach said that because I didn't see HOW things could actually get worse because they were ALREADY TERRIBLE.

And that's when Mr Graves shouted into the megaphone, "IT'S TIME FOR THE FINAL GAME. GET READY FOR THE ALL-STAFF EGG-AND-SPOON RACE!"

We watched as all the teachers RAN over to the STARTING LINE with their eggs and spoons.

And Jodi said, "This is about to get even MORE SERIOUS. Look."

She pointed and we saw the OFFICE LADIES marching down the stairs and out into the playground.

Then the dining-hall doors BURST OPEN and the DINNER LADIES came RUNNING OUT and they had their POTS AND PANS and they were BANGING THEM with their ICE-CREAM SCOOPS, and they ran across the playground towards us!

We watched as all the TEACHERS and OFFICE LADIES and CLASSROOM ASSISTANTS and DINNER LADIES and CARETAKERS and the LIBRARIAN and the LOLLIPOP MAN stood on the starting line ready to race.

Loads of them were pulling at their ARMS and LEGS and doing WARM-UPS and the dinner ladies were STILL banging their POTS and PANS.

Then Mr Graves yelled, "Ready... Steady..."

And Laser Linghams grabbed the megaphone off him and screamed, "GO,"

and the dinner ladies THREW down their
pots and everyone started to run!

We tried to keep up with who was
WINNING but it was really hard because
EVERYONE was running so fast that there
was GRASS and MUD and EGGS flying
EVERYWHERE.

And LOADS of people were screaming
"MY EGG!" and "NOOOOOOOOOO!" and
some of them were even trying to scoop up
bits of BROKEN SHELL and RAW EGG on
to their spoons!

People were SCREAMING and some of
them were kneeling on the ground CRYING

and Mr Killington actually even ripped his T-SHIRT in HALF when he dropped his egg!

There was MUD and BROKEN EGGS EVERYWHERE.

But then Jodi said, "LOOK!"

And I looked and saw that Miss Jones and Miss Veil were the only ones left in the race because the dinner ladies that were still running didn't have eggs OR spoons and were just waving their ice-cream scoops about instead!

Jodi grabbed my hand and SQUEEZED TIGHT and I held my breath because I knew that this was SUPER IMPORTANT and that whoever won THIS race was going to be our TEACHER. And that the other one was going to get SACKED FOR LIFE or WORSE.

That's when Zach grabbed my OTHER hand and I looked and saw that he had his eyes SHUT TIGHT.

Then, all of a sudden, there was SCREAMING and we saw Miss Veil lying on the ground with her egg SMASHED next to her and Miss Jones was crossing the finishing line with her egg still in ONE PIECE.

Zach picked me up and started jumping

up and down and Jodi was whistling in that
REALLY LOUD WAY her mum taught her
to do and Maisie was actually CRYING with
HAPPINESS.

That's when Jessi STORMED over to us
and she did NOT look happy.

And she looked RIGHT at Maisie and said,
"You picked the WRONG SIDE, Maisie
Miller!"

And she looked at the rest of us and said,
"This. Isn't. OVER."

DEFINITELY NOT A DINOSAUR!

The next morning we noticed that all the St Balthazar's pupils were acting WEIRD.

Jodi kept getting up and pretending that she needed to sharpen her PENCIL so that she could walk past Jessi's table, but every time she got NEAR them they stopped talking and just LOOKED at her.

And then, all of a sudden, Maisie said, "I remember. I got it wrong. Izzy, I remember now!"

And then, before I could stop her, she GRABBED Jodi's backpack and RAN out of the classroom!

I gasped and looked round and I could see that Miss Jones and Miss Veil were having an ARGUMENT in the STORE CUPBOARD about how Miss Veil had CHANGED the laptop SCREENSAVER from a photo of a DOG to a photo of a CAT, and it seemed quite SERIOUS because

they'd been in there for AGES.

So that's when I decided to take a risk, and I got up and ran after Maisie all the way to The Den even though my heart was POUNDING.

I BURST through the door and saw Maisie sitting on the floor flicking through the LATIN DICTIONARY she'd taken from Jodi's bag.

I shut the door behind me and sat down on the floor and said, "Maisie, we need to be quick! We'll be in deep trouble if the teachers notice we've left!"

But Maisie wasn't listening.

She was STARING at the dictionary.

And then she looked up at me and said, "It wasn't 'LACTRODACTAL'. I remembered it wrong. But I remember now. It was 'LACTRODECTUS'."

I stared at Maisie, waiting for her to tell me what it meant.

But then, all of a sudden, there was a SCREAM outside The Den!

So we rushed out into the corridor and THAT'S when we saw the Year 3 teacher RUNNING out of her classroom and down the corridor, yelling, "SPIDERS! MY DESK IS FULL OF SPIDERS! HELP!"

I looked at Maisie and her eyes were actually SHAKING.

So I took a deep breath to calm myself and said, "'LACTRODECTUS' means 'SPIDER', doesn't it?"

And that's when Maisie looked up at me and said, "No."

And then she said, "It means BLACK WIDOW SPIDER."

I GASPED and said, "We need to EVACUATE THE SCHOOL!"

And Maisie nodded.

Because we knew that BLACK WIDOW SPIDERS are one of the most POISONOUS

spiders in the WORLD.

So that's when I tucked my TROUSERS into my SOCKS and put Maisie on my BACK because her eyes had started to go all SWIRLY. And then I ran into the Year 3 classroom and shouted,

"EVACUATE! EVACUATE!"

And all the Year 3s came RUNNING out because we're in Year 4, so if I say they have to do something, they do it because we are the OLDER ONES.

And then I ran into the next classroom and the next and did the same until I got to the end of the corridor. But then I realised that it was going to take TOO LONG to go into all the classrooms and shout "EVACUATE" and that a BLACK WIDOW SPIDER could ATTACK at

ANY MOMENT.

So that's when I had to make a decision. A **BIG** decision. The type of decision that you can actually get

EXPELLED

from school for **LIFE** for making! But I had to do it to save everyone's life and stop the **NEW PUPILS** from

DESTROYING US ALL

with their FLIES and BLACK WIDOW
SPIDERS and from taking over OUR
SCHOOL.

Spiders, Floods and Fire

I ran to the fire alarm at the bottom of the stairs that go up to our classroom and put Maisie down for a second so I could catch my BREATH. But as SOON as her feet touched the floor I heard a SPLASH and Maisie SCREAMED.

And that's when we saw that there was WATER pouring down the STAIRS!

Then, all of a sudden, we heard SCREAMING and SPLASHING and Jodi and Zach and some of the St Balthazar's pupils appeared at the top of the stairs.

And Jodi shouted, "FLOOD! GET OUT!"

So I shouted, "BLACK WIDOW SPIDERS! GET OUT MORE!!"

Jessi and the new pupils GASPED and she pointed RIGHT AT ME and did NOT look happy!

So that's when I told Maisie to cover her ears TIGHT. And then I hit the fire alarm and we RAN.

We all knew that the new pupils were FURIOUS with us for ruining their BLACK WIDOW SPIDER ATTACK.

Zach said that he was a bit SCARED of them now and that maybe we should HIDE in case they threw a SPIDER at us!

That's when Jodi said that HIDING was a

GOOD IDEA

and that we could SPY ON THEM to find out what they were going to do next.

So we all climbed up on top of the old bike shed and watched as a big group of ST BALTHAZAR'S PUPILS huddled together away from everyone else, and then they all TOUCHED their BLAZER BADGES and started CHANTING.

That's when Zach GASPED and said, "I don't think they're just a secret society. I think they've got POWERS!"

Then Zach said that he thought their CHANTING had made things APPEAR. Like FLIES and WATER and SPIDERS.

And he turned and looked at us and said, "I think they're about to do something else!"

Then, all of a sudden, a BIG WHITE VAN pulled up outside the school gates, next to where the pupils were standing, and all the new pupils RUSHED over.

That's when Jodi got up on her knees so she could get a better look.

And Maisie squealed, "GET DOWN!
THEY'LL SEE!"

But Jodi DIDN'T get down.

She said, "There could be ANYTHING
inside that van! It might be a van full of
venomous SNAKES for all we know and
they're about to set them LOOSE in the
playground! We have to do something!"

So that's when we all sneaked down from
the bike shed and ran along the side of the
playground keeping close to the wall AT
ALL TIMES, just like Jodi had trained us
to do, until we got near enough to see what
was going on.

THAT'S when we saw two people with a **TV CAMERA** get out of the van. And one of them took out a **MICROPHONE** and stuck it through the school railing and pointed it at the new pupils and asked them if they could tell her what was happening at the school.

And **THAT'S** when we heard Jessi say, "It's a **DEEPLY** unsafe and unhygienic school. I can't believe they sent us here instead of keeping St Balthazar's open! We're all scared for our **LIVES!**"

All the new pupils nodded their heads and made these **REALLY FAKE** scared looks.

Then the lady pointed the microphone at

Zavier and said, "Can you tell me exactly what happened here today?"

But Jessi butted in and said, "The dining hall is INFESTED with INSECTS and we were all served food covered in FLIES. Then one of the teachers found hundreds of

POISONOUS BLACK WIDOW SPIDERS

in her desk, which means they're probably nesting ALL OVER the school. Then the toilets exploded because they are old and DIRTY and now the school is FLOODED

and everything is SMELLY and RUINED. Oh, and I think part of the school might be ON FIRE now too!"

The reporter looked absolutely

and she just sort of STARED at Jessi for a bit, then she said, "Is there anything else you'd like to tell us?"

And that's when Jessi said, "Yes, actually. I saw a RAT."

And that's when Jodi GASPED and walked away from the wall into CLEAR VIEW and yelled, "Don't you mean a RATTUS?!"

Jessi turned around and she

GASPED.

Then Jodi stepped even CLOSER and said, "That's right. We know about the SECRET LATIN. And your CHANTING. We know EXACTLY who you are. All of you!"

The reporter pulled the mic away from the new pupils and put it on the end of a LONG STICK and stuck it through the railings again in front of Jodi's face and said, "And who ARE they?"

And that's when Jodi said, "They're an

EVIL SECRET SOCIETY.

They have secret HANDSHAKES and secret SYMBOLS and a secret-society BLAZER and they have secret-society MEETINGS where they only speak in LATIN. And they've come here to DESTROY US and take over our school!"

And that's when Zach walked over and stood next to Jodi and said, "YEAH! And they have POWERS too!"

The reporter looked a bit annoyed and she said, "Powers?"

And that's when Zach said that they could make things like SPIDERS and WATER appear and that they probably had special SHOE-SHINING POWERS too! Then HE pointed at their shoes and said, "I mean, look at how shiny they are! That's not normal!"

And that's when the reporter pulled her microphone away and said, "There's no story here. Just a bunch of kids messing about." And then she told the cameraman to stop filming and they both got back in the van and drove away.

Then **ALL** the St Balthazar's pupils turned and **GLARED** at us. And they looked

MEGA ANGRY.

And Jessi said, "Why did you tell them that we're a secret society? With

POWERS?!"

And Jodi crossed her arms and said, "So that the **WORLD FINDS OUT!**"

And another pupil said, "But we're **NOT** a secret society!"

So that's when I took a deep breath and stepped forward and said, "Except that you ARE!"

And that's when Jessi smiled. But it didn't look as creepy as it had before.

And then she said, "You really think we have POWERS?"

Then she burst out LAUGHING and so did all the other new pupils!

That's when I could FEEL my hands and arms SHAKING and I wasn't sure if it was because I was SCARED or ANGRY or BOTH.

And I said, "So it wasn't YOU who put the FLIES in the school dinners? And made up the story about rats? And FLOODED the school? And planted the BLACK WIDOW SPIDERS?"

And that's when Jessi didn't reply because she knew that they'd been CAUGHT. Then she got a bit of a weird look on her face and all the others started looking at each other and I could **TELL** that they were getting a bit **WORRIED.**

And Jodi said, "We'll be telling **EVERYONE**. You're a secret society and you're trying to **DESTROY US** and take over our school for yourself!"

But Jessi shook her head and said, "Is that what you think? You've got it all wrong! I **PROMISE** you we don't want your school for ourselves!

"What we're really trying to do is

DESTROY IT!"

DESTROY
THIS
SCHOOL!

Once Mr Graves realised that the spiders were FAKE and there was NO FIRE, everyone was allowed an EXTENDED BREAK while the PLUMBERS came to fix the BURST PIPE in the toilet.

So that's when we SNUCK BACK into the

school to go to The Den for an

EMERGENCY MEETING.

But Jessi and Zavier followed us!

Jessi stopped us outside the door and said, "Look. We're sorry, OK? Don't tell anyone what we did. We'll get in trouble. The flies were just normal flies that we collected from the compost site at our old school and the spiders were fake, obviously. And I have no idea who set off the fire alarm but it wasn't us!"

Maisie gasped and said, "But you're trying to **DESTROY** our school!"

And that's when Jessi and Zavier looked at each other, but they didn't say anything.

So **THAT'S** when Jodi said that if they didn't tell us **EVERYTHING RIGHT NOW** she was going to tell the teachers what they'd done.

And Jessi said, "**FINE**."

So that's how we found out that they wanted to destroy our school just enough that it got **CLOSED** and the council had to **REOPEN** St Balthazar's so that they would get to go back.

And Zach said, "Where are WE meant to go if our school gets closed down? Did you think about that?"

But Jessi and Zavier didn't say anything – they just looked down at their shoes again.

Then Jodi said, "What is the CHANTING about if you're NOT a secret society?"

And that's when Zavier laughed a bit and said that the CHANTING was just them singing their OLD SCHOOL SONG that was in LATIN and that they were doing it to make them happy because they didn't like being here and they wanted to go back to their old school.

And then he looked RIGHT at Jodi and said, "And YOU lot can't talk about secret societies! You've GOT ONE!"

And Jodi looked

SHOCKED

and she said, "What? No, we don't!"

And Zavier said, "I've seen you all making your EYES go WIDE at each other. It's a SIGNAL. And then you run off to your DEN. I even watched you do ARMY MOVES when you snuck up on us earlier! You've got your own secret society, so you've no right to say we have when we don't."

And Jodi didn't say anything and neither did ANY of us because he was sort of RIGHT.

That's when Zach said, "The Latin is a bit creepy, though, don't you think?"

And that's when they all laughed and Daisy said, "We like it. It's been our school song for one hundred and fifty years!"

And we all looked at each other and Zach said, "WOW" because we had no idea how OLD St Balthazar's had been!

Then Jodi asked about them being in The Den and spying on us and stealing our notebook! And that's when Jessi said, "We were looking for something."

And Jodi said, "What?"

And Jessi gave Zavier a look and Zavier said, "The trophy."

We all STARED at each other when Zavier said that because we had

why they thought that the trophy THEY STOLE would be in OUR den!

Then Zavier looked at Jessi, and Jessi said, "We heard a rumour."

Jodi narrowed her eyes and said, "What rumour?"

And that's when Zavier said, "Jessi heard someone say that your school only PRETENDED that the trophy was stolen so that you could BLAME US because you've always hated us!"

And then Jodi gasped and said, "That's not true! YOUR SCHOOL hates OUR SCHOOL because we won!"

That's when I said, "And that doesn't explain why you took our notebook."

And Jessi looked down at the ground and Zavier explained that they knew we had

a secret club and that they overheard us talking about them and that they wanted to know what we were saying in case we knew about their

PLAN to DESTROY

our school.

That's when Jodi said, "Give it back then. Now."

And Jessi took it out of her bag and handed it to Jodi.

Then Jodi said, "I'm sorry about your old school, but I'm afraid your plan has failed.

You'll **NEVER** destroy our school. Not as long as **WE'RE** here!"

And Maisie said, "If everyone could just forget about the **TROPHY THING** everything would be fine and we could all be friends!"

And then she said that the St Balthazar's pupils were

JUST LIKE US

and that they liked solving stuff and knew loads of stuff about the **POLICE** and **INVESTIGATIONS** and that Jessi and Jodi

were basically the SAME PERSON.

And then she BEGGED everyone to forget about THE INCIDENT and being ARCH-ENEMIES.

But Jodi shouted, "NEVER. They STOLE our trophy!"

And Jessi shouted, "NO, WE DIDN'T!"

And then someone said, "Excuse me, but you lot need to move away from here," and we saw that BUILDERS were taking down one of the wooden panels blocking up the entrance to the OLD WING.

And that's when Zach said, "Wait. What's that?!"

Before we could STOP him, Zach went into the OLD WING and we saw him looking into a box with something BIG and SILVER sticking out of it.

And then he held it up and everyone

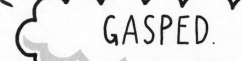

GASPED.

Because it was a TROPHY.

And it wasn't just ANY trophy.

It was THE TROPHY! The STOLEN TROPHY!

And that's when Jessi yelled,

"SEE! I TOLD YOU WE DIDN'T STEAL IT!"

Destroying Our School TOGETHER!

None of us could believe that the trophy had been here all along and that it hadn't been stolen by St Balthazar's years ago like we'd all thought.

And that's when Zach said, "So you're **NOT** our arch-enemies!"

EVERYONE was in SHOCK and NO ONE knew why the trophy had been left in the OLD WING when it had been boarded up, but it had obviously been a MISTAKE. A really BIG mistake!

Then Jodi said, "I can't believe it's been in there all this time!"

And that's when Jessi said, "YUP."

And she had her hands on her hips, but she looked a bit upset in her face like she was going to CRY, and I didn't know if they were ANGRY TEARS or SAD TEARS or **BOTH**. And that's when I realised that we owed Jessi and **EVERYONE** from St Balthazar's's a **HUGE APOLOGY**.

I didn't know if they were **EVER** going to be able to **FORGIVE US** or if they would **HATE US FOREVER**. But I knew that we were going to have to do something

BIG

to show them that we'd got it all wrong and that we were sorry.

So that's when I said, "We're sorry. And we're going to make it up to you."

And EVERYONE looked at me.

And then Jessi said, "Yeah? HOW?"

And I took a deep breath and said, "We're going to help you destroy our school!"

Everyone stopped GASPING and started SMILING when I explained what I meant and told them about my

BIG IDEA.

I thought we should DESTROY our school so that it wasn't just OUR school any more. We needed it to be a NEW SCHOOL because that's what we were now.

Maisie got

and she started saying **LOADS** of stuff about how the St Balthazar's's school song could become **OUR** school song because we didn't have one anyway. But that maybe we could change the music just a little bit so it wasn't as **CREEPY** and everyone laughed.

That's when Zavier said, "**OK**. We're in!"

And I said that we could make a NEW SCHOOL BADGE and that it could be a mix of BOTH our school badges. Or that we could make a BRAND-NEW ONE together.

And Jodi smiled, and I could tell that she liked that idea.

And then Jessi said, "Well, if you really mean it, I think that sounds quite cool actually."

And that's when Maisie

SCREAMED WITH HAPPINESS

and then she took her old blazer out of her
bag and put it back on and

PUNCHED

the air and we
all laughed.

A VERY Special Announcement

It took **AGES** for the council to **EVENTUALLY** respond to our letter and I think that the only reason they got back to us was because we sent **ANOTHER** letter threatening to do a **PROTEST** about the **FIRST LETTER** not being answered.

When we got a reply, Mr Graves called a big assembly because he was still our head teacher because LASER LINGHAMS had been asked to go and teach in FLORIDA in AMERICA and when she told us all Mr Graves had looked really UPSET that HE wasn't the one going to Florida!

And because our school was

SO BIG

now that the OLD WING was open, we got to keep ALL our teachers AND the St Balthazar's teachers, so that was good and it

meant we didn't have to have another FUN DAY.

Once we were all sitting down and listening quietly, Mr Graves said, "I have a very, VERY special announcement. I'd like to call up the pupils who came up with the idea and made it happen. So, everyone, would you please put your hands together for our very first PUPIL COUNCIL!"

And I couldn't BELIEVE that Mr Graves had just said that because WE were the brand-new pupil council, which meant that WE had to go up on stage and that WE had to tell everyone about the reply we'd got

from the council!

So that's when Jodi squeezed my hand and said,

"LET'S GO!"

So me and Jodi and Maisie and Zach got up and started to walk up the little steps. And Zach even did a bit of a marching thing like the St Balthazar's pupils had done the first day they came and EVERYONE laughed.

And then Jessi and Zavier got up on stage too and everyone CHEERED. And then Mr Graves handed Jodi the microphone. And then she gave it to ME and WINKED, and I was a bit SHOCKED because I didn't expect her to do that!

So that's when I said, "Um. Hi, everyone. Thanks for filling out the questionnaire and signing the petition."

And then I handed the microphone to Jessi because she was the one who had said we should START a PUPIL COUNCIL because there'd been one at her old school. Also she was a bit more used to being on stage than I was and I wasn't really sure what to say next!

So Jessi took the microphone and said,

"The council AGREED to us choosing a new name for our school OURSELVES, so we took your suggestions and counted the votes and we can now confirm LIVE that our new school is called..."

That's when everyone started banging their feet like a

DRUM ROLL.

Jessi handed the microphone to Maisie and Maisie held it REALLY CLOSE to her mouth and yelled,

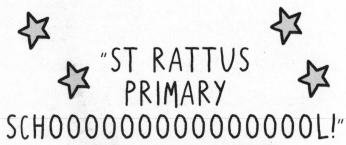

"ST RATTUS PRIMARY SCHOOOOOOOOOOOOOOOOOL!"

And everyone went

WILD!

Acknowledgements

Huge thanks to my brilliant editor, Kirsty.
SO appreciate your help with this one! And thank
you to everyone at Nosy Crow who worked so
hard to get this one out in time!

Love and pugs to Tom for the fantastic
illustrations. You're awesome!

And THANK YOU to the lovely indie
bookseller Sue Porter at Linghams Booksellers
(aka Laser Linghams!) who let me steal her
name AND her LASER EYES for this book.

MORE love, pugs and thanks to my awesome agent,
Becky. I am eternally grateful for everything you do!

Most of all, thank you to my amazing wee boy, Albie.
You make Mummy SO HAPPY. And that helps
me (try!) to be funny. I love you.